Rain Man,

Lies He Told:
Book Two

SYLVIE GRAYSON

For information contact:

GREAT WESTERN PUBLISHING at
sylviegraysonauthor@gmail.com

Copyright © 2020 by Sylvie Grayson

All rights reserved.

ISBN: 978-1-989491-00-3

Great Western Publishing is a registered trademark of Sylvie Grayson.

Cover art by Covers by Kay
https://www.facebook.com/coversbykay/

Praise for Sylvie Grayson's books

I've been reading Sylvie Grayson - can't seem to put them down. How do you come up with these exciting mysteries? Very fun reading!!

Suspended Animation

Wow! This book is amazing, its very well written and the characters are very well developed. This is my first book by Sylvie Grayson and it won't be my last. I was hooked from the first page and this book was very hard to put down.

Interesting characters, family conflicts and divided loyalties make this a book that kept me up half the night

Legal Obstruction

I loved this book! I've found my new favorite author. Emily is a fiercely professional woman who is on her own and determined to protect her little family. Joe is a solitary guy who often doesn't deal with problems until they are front and center. But boy does Emily wake him up and does he take notice. Add in a wildcard assistant and a few unsavory characters and I was up all night finishing the book to find out what happens.

The Lies He Told Me

If you are a fan of the heartwarming craftiness and domesticity of a Debbie McComber romance, and the intense intrigues of Danielle Steele, you'll enjoy the writing style of Sylvie Grayson; where the bad guys are not heartless, and the good guys are virtually flawless.

Just a quick note to let you know how much I enjoyed your book. You drew on your vast experience as a result of being a female, a wife, lover, mother, business woman, lawyer, friend, gardener, homeowner, compassionate and

Books by Sylvie Grayson

Romantic suspense

Suspended Animation

Legal Obstruction

Lies He Told Me, book one

Moon Shine

Dead Wrong

False Confession

My Best Mistake

Prairie Storm

Romantic suspense in a sci/fi fantasy world of The Last War

Khandarken Rising, Book One

Son of the Emperor, Book Two

Truth and Treachery, Book Three

Weapon of Tyrants, Book Four

Prince of Jiran, Book Five

Banderos, Book Six

The Last Sovereign, Book Seven

caring individual. It was an intriguing read which kept me guessing and very interested. Well done, Sylvie.

The Last War: Book One, Khandarken Rising
The General of Khandarken sends his son, Dante, to investigate the situation. When Dante meets the lovely Beth she eyes him with suspicion. But he won't stop until he solves the tangle of motives, fueled by greed, which threaten Beth and her family. I enjoyed this book very much. The well-developed characters and sensuous love scenes make this a page turner. I look forward to reading Book Two and Book Three

... this story is one of a kind in its own and couldn't be truly compared to anything but itself. It has so many unique characteristics to it. The personal relationships are intriguing and different from many other fictional relationships. The names are cool, the plot gets thicker with each page, and I loved the author's style. It became evident that I was addicted to reading the book once I was sad to be finished. I'm going to give this a strong recommendation. It's my kind of book.

The Last War: Book Two, Son of the Emperor
I am a big fan of The Last War series. I loved Book One, the story of Major Dante Regiment and Beth Farmer. The dystopian world Grayson has created, where women are scarce and Clones are used to replace them, where the Emperor has finally been defeated but his son takes up the fight, just gets better in this second book. ...Thrills abound on the race to freedom and home. I really enjoyed this book and can't wait for Book Three. Grayson has great imagination, the fantasy series is awesome.

Truth and Treachery, The Last War: Book Three
4 stars - Format: Paperback

Ok, this series is just getting better and better. The increasing complexity of the characters and the development of lead characters is a pleasure to read. The plot, with its twists and turns, intrigue and adventure, is a real joy. If you liked the first two books in The Last War series (and, seriously, that's the place to start before reading this book - it's worth doing) then you will love this book.

Weapon of Tyrants, The Last War: Book Four
4 stars

The Last War has been a truly excellent series so far, and Weapon of Tyrants is staying strong. Exciting, full of intrigue and adventure, wonderfully developed strong lead characters with a great supporting cast, neat world-building and excellent writing. I mean, what more can you ask for? You do need to start with book 1 in this series, but it too was excellent so you can't go wrong, and I can guarantee you'll have a ball with this one when you reach it.

DEDICATION

I am blessed with wonderful support that has enabled me to write. To my husband, who gives me the freedom to work but is always ready to listen, read and lend a hand with difficult passages. To my children who had faith in me and helped with their support and practical suggestions, the choosing of titles and cover art.

To my critique group—who all supported me to polish the words for publication, my many thanks.

Any errors or omissions are mine alone.

Sylvie Grayson

www.sylviegrayson.com

https://www.bookbub.com/profile/sylvie-grayson

sylviegraysonauthor@gmail.com

https://www.facebook.com/sylvie.grayson

.

Rain Man

Lies He Told: Book Two

SYLVIE GRAYSON

CHAPTER ONE

At least they didn't put him in jail. Rainier Murdoch couldn't think of anything that would embarrass his folks more. They were still shaken by what they'd learned during the court hearings and probation negotiations about his activities in the past. At first the police were going to charge him with murder as well as tax evasion, but he'd been able to prove that charge was unsupported by the facts. Surprisingly, it had been a relief to be caught and deal with the whole mess after months of working undercover and running from the police. His business partner was dead, and when the dust settled Rain was charged with running a gambling operation without a license and failure to pay the taxes on the proceeds. Now he was on probation, having managed to avoid spending time in the clink.

Rain pulled his pickup to the side of the rural road and parked in the empty gravelled area he'd found here before. Early spring, and the sun was shining glaringly on the fast receding water in the flats. He reached for his binoculars in the glove box and climbed out to walk to the edge of the pond. Uncle Toby had a house on the other side of the open water and there wasn't a better place in Victoria to watch the birds. Since moving to Vancouver Island from the Canadian Prairies, he'd missed the wildlife he'd grown up with in Saskatchewan.

Once he discovered this viewpoint, he'd been able to identify so many species—trumpeter swans, although their tenure in the winter was brief, Canada Geese, which stuck around all year long and raised their goslings here once the water dried up, numerous types of ducks, and of course the ubiquitous coastal gulls. Overhead flew the predator birds—bald eagles, red-tail hawks, sharp-shinned hawks, turkey vultures. He figured there must be a crow rookery nearby, because he'd often seen hordes of them flying in noisy formation, usually chasing the eagles who raided their nests in the spring.

The flats were quiet today, the shallow water still, a dozen large grey and black geese floating calmly in a circle near the middle of the pond. Through the trees, he caught sight of the deck of Uncle Toby's house. He scanned the view with his binoculars, pausing in surprise at what he saw. He'd been on that deck a few times with his uncle, there were a shower and a hot tub positioned there. Uncle Toby would pour him a scotch, toss him a towel and lead the way out the door where they'd each have a quick shower and step into the steaming water to relax and catch up with each other.

Someone was showering on the deck. He adjusted the lenses of his binoculars and took a closer look as his breath caught in his throat. It was a woman, young from the look of her, although her face wasn't what held his total attention. As the water flowed over her shapely body, she soaped up then lifted an arm to rinse, her breast moving enticingly with the motion. She turned to wash her other side and he focussed on her ass. *Very nice.*

This wasn't any business of his. Toby could entertain whomever he wanted at his place. He was a widower, after all, and not dating anyone Rain was aware of. Rainier glanced around in sudden worry to see who else might be watching the activity on the deck. There was no one here but himself which caused the tension in his chest to ease somewhat.

The problem was, Uncle Toby had left town last week. Having finally retired from the Royal Canadian Mounted Police, the national police force, he'd taken a long talked about trip to southeast Asia. The house should be empty. Had this person just steered down his road, walked onto the deck to shower and use his hot tub? As Rain watched, the woman leaned to shut off the showerhead and flipped the lid of the hot tub open. Then she stepped in, steam rising in a cloud around her.

What to do? Toby hadn't specifically asked him to keep an eye on the house. Should he just ignore this? Since being charged with the criminal offences, Rainier had been released on bail. The conditions of his probation included working with the cops on various cases where they thought his skills would be of use. As time went by, he'd begun to feel like a police officer, given some kind of responsibility to enforce the law. Spending time with Uncle Toby in the last few months had simply reinforced that feeling. He couldn't walk past this.

Lowering the binoculars, he headed determinedly for his truck. In Rain's previous life, he'd changed cars yearly to maintain his undercover status, buying them with cash and using a different ID each time to purchase and register the vehicle. This truck had been with him longer than any single vehicle in years. He was slowly getting used to the idea that he didn't have to move fast and cover his tracks anymore. Instead, he could settle down to a regular life like most other people. His job today was to find out what was going on at Uncle Toby's place. Getting a closer look at the woman with the great ass and spectacular chest would just be a bonus.

When Rain pulled up in front of Uncle Toby's door, everything looked normal. Toby's truck was parked in its usual spot in the drive, where he'd left it when he took off for his travels. He never used the twin garages attached to the side of the house, and on Rain's first tour of the place, he'd noticed they were full of junk, so no room to fit his vehicle in there. Either the female visitor was driving Toby's truck, or she'd left her car elsewhere. But she had to have access to a vehicle of some kind, out here in the boonies.

Parking right in front of the entry, he climbed out, slamming his door loudly. Didn't want to startle anyone unnecessarily. Marching up the couple of steps to the front door, he pressed his thumb hard on the button for the doorbell. It chimed inside the house.

There was the sound of footsteps approaching, but the door didn't open right away. He turned his face toward the side window, imagining he was being scrutinized by the occupant within. That probably meant they were nervous about having a caller show up at the door. The question was, would they open it?

Then he heard the lock snick back and saw the handle twist down. The door opened, and his heart beat a little harder. Would it be Toby or the woman he'd seen on the back deck?

He spotted a pair of bare feet, the toenails painted a dark red, and his gaze travelled up slim bare legs to the hem of a silky-looking green housecoat. There was enticing cleavage where the garment met across the woman's chest. Her face was lovely, pale blue eyes and a plump mouth. A smile formed on that exquisite face. "Hello, Rain Man," she said. "I've been waiting for you."

***

CHAPTER TWO

Standing in her father's doorway, Sophia watched as Rain's jaw dropped. "Thea Sophia?" he croaked.

Her smile widened. At least he remembered her. She'd been worried he'd been gone too long from where they grew up together on the Prairies to recall their childhood drama. "I go by Sophia now," she said.

"I just saw your father before he left," he replied cautiously. "Uncle Toby didn't mention you were coming to town."

"I didn't know I was, and nor did he," she said. "It was a last-minute decision. Come in. I'll take a moment to get dressed."

"Did you just get up?" he asked, with an idiotic look on his face.

"No, I was in the hot tub out on the deck. It's wonderful, you should try it."

"I have, with your Dad," He nodded as his face turned bright red. "It is nice, very relaxing. Do you have a vehicle or are you using Toby's truck?"

Startled, she shot him a hesitant look. Giving out too much information would be a bad idea in the circumstances in which she found herself. Things were already tenuous for her and with Dad out of the country she felt somewhat vulnerable. "I've got my own car but it's in the garage."

He smiled, that beautiful open expression she remembered so well. "Whew," he said. "How'd you manage that? Last time I looked they were both chock full."

She laughed, watching his cheeks go dark. "I know. Dad had to work pretty hard to make room for my car. Luckily, I caught him just before he left town."

She waved him toward the living room and went down the hall in the direction of the bedrooms. Rain was here! She felt like doing a little happy dance in the hallway. He looked the same, just a little older, tougher. His mouth was tight, his jaw tense. She was aware of some of the recent events in his life– Dad had kept the family informed. It couldn't have been easy for Rain to handle everything that had happened, especially the death of his friend and business partner, Jeff Sanderson.

Sophia remembered from years ago when Jeff showed up at their high school in Moose Jaw, Saskatchewan. She'd been in grade nine, the same as Rain's brother Jake. Rain and Jeff were starting grade eleven together. Jeff was a tall redhead with an easy-going, sophisticated manner and he and Rain fell into a fast friendship. Sophia had been unimpressed by him. She thought he was charming but shallow. Jeff's father had worked in the oil industry all over the world – Chile, Japan, Norway—but this time he'd been posted to a refinery in Saskatchewan. When the boys graduated from high school, they took off together for the west coast, and Sophia had been heartbroken that Rain was gone. Now here he was in her father's living room. A little flutter took up space in her stomach.

Moving quickly, she entered her room. She had taken possession of the bedroom nearest her father's when she'd arrived, nervous and tense from her evasive travels. Dad had been surprised but glad to see her. Right away, he thought she must be in trouble and hesitated to go on his long-planned trip to Southeast Asia. He'd been worried about leaving her here alone. But she'd lied, insisting she had everything under control. He'd believed her, given that keeping things under control had been Job One for her ever since mother died when she was fourteen.

And now Rain had arrived. Dad promised Rainier Murdoch would show up. He said if Rainier didn't come after a few days, he'd get hold of him and send him out to see her. Already, because of his presence, the tension she'd long held tight in her shoulders was starting to ease.

~~~

Rain wandered into the kitchen overlooking the back deck. He rubbed sweating hands down the legs of his jeans. Thea Sophia Bonnar was here in her father's home. Why was he so surprised? He'd been caught off balance, suddenly seeing her like this. The image he held in his head of the woman showering on the deck made him distinctly uncomfortable, now that he realized who it was. Rain had spent years avoiding contact with the Bonnar kids— they broke his heart.

He glanced out the window. The bird feeders on the back deck were still full. Toby liked to look after the birds when he was home. One of the feeders swung wildly as a flurry of juncos departed, fluttering into the huge fir tree beside the house. A fat male towhee dropped noisily onto the plastic lid of the feeder, scaring away all the other birds. Its mate tweeted at him from the spiraea bush below the railing, hopping from branch to branch as she waited her turn.

Then he heard a low feminine voice calling from the hallway. "Where did you go? Oh, here you are." Sophia appeared in the kitchen doorway, wearing tight jeans and a loose top that draped enticingly across her small frame, outlining her breasts. Wow. He didn't remember her being so well endowed. She'd changed since last he'd laid eyes on her, or at least since last he was willing to pay any attention.

When they were younger, he'd worked hard not to notice her. Dad and Toby Bonnar were buddies, they had met up in the Canadian military during the Korean War activity and stayed close after discharge from the army, both moving to the wide Canadian Prairies at the same time and buying up land for their farms. Thus the *Uncle* Toby. They weren't really related, but with farms next door to each other on the outskirts of Moose Jaw, they'd worked together and played together. Their children grew up together, especially after Aunt Thea Sophia died.

There were three children in the Murdoch family—Susan, their older sister, who was married now with a little girl, Rainier, and Jacob the youngest boy. Jake was the thorn in his side that young Rain loved to hate. But Toby and Thea Sophia Bonnar had six kids. Sophia was second oldest. There was an older boy, also Toby, then four more little ones after her, the youngest only about three when the mother died. Her loss had devastated the family.

"Did Dad get hold of you?" Sophia asked him now.

Rain dragged his gaze from her chest to her face, frowning in annoyance that he might have been caught ogling her. "No, why? Did he have something to tell me?"

"I don't know. Just wondered why you're here if you knew he left last week." Her cheeks had gone pale.

Heat rose up his chest to suffuse his face. "To be honest, I was over there." He turned and pointed out the kitchen window across the flats to the road on the other side. "I was watching the birds and noticed motion on the deck. There appeared to be someone in the hot tub."

"Oh." Her face was no longer pale but had turned a burning red, and he hastily reassured her, while lying through his teeth. "I knew Toby was out of town and he didn't tell me anyone would be staying in the house. I thought I should check it out, make sure the house hadn't been broken into or something."

"Okay." She nodded, unable to meet his gaze. "Dad said I could stay here."

He waved that away. "Of course he did. I just didn't know it was family."

"Right. Well, he's lucky he's got someone onside who's keeping an eye out for him. He didn't tell me."

"Hmm." Rain rubbed the neglected stubble on his jaw. "Are you staying here the whole time he's away? Because it's pretty isolated for a single woman alone."

"I know. He's got an alarm system, right?"

"Sure he does. Show me how it works." He turned and headed toward the front door, leaving her to trail behind him.

"You think I don't know how to set it?" she demanded indignantly of his back, her voice rising in frustration.

He stifled a grin. Thea Sophia hadn't changed.

***

CHAPTER THREE

Rainier walked into the headquarters of the Victoria RCMP detachment near Victoria's downtown. His appointment was with Detective Ross Cullen. He'd received a notification the day before. There was a new case and Rain's contribution to the investigation was, as always, to follow the money. This was the part of his probation that put him most in conflict with himself. Hiding the money had been his job when he worked with Jeff Sanderson, his old buddy and business partner. Rain collected the money from the online betting sites he created and managed, siphoning it in cash over to Jeff. Jeff's part was to put the funds to work. Thus the commercial building Rain now co-owned with Jeff's widow, Chloe. Chloe had married Ross Cullen some time after Jeff died— things were a bit complicated. But when Jeff was killed, their whole operation had been thrown into chaos. Rain had been impressed with the way Chloe held things together for her little family after that life-changing event.

He gave his name at reception, and soon Ross came thundering down the stairs to meet him and take him up to his office. *Office* wasn't quite the right word. Cullen worked in a little cubicle on the second floor, files scattered all over the surface of his desk and stacked on a set of plastic shelves behind him. The detective positioned himself at his desk, and Rain took the only other seat available, a creaky chair with wobbly legs opposite him.

"Thanks for coming in, Murdoch," Ross said, clearing his throat. "This one's probably right up your alley. The case has been open for a while with little success so we're all hoping for some progress. I'm anxious to see what you can do with it."

Rain nodded. "Okay," he said. "I'll do what I can."

Ross glinted a smile at him. "I know you will, that's what your probation conditions say."

Heat flooded his neck. He was still not comfortable with being a convicted felon. Would he ever be? This conviction wasn't going to go away. It was called a record for a reason.

Ross shifted in his chair and flipped open the top folder on his desk. "Here's what we have." His thick finger followed a typed list on the first sheet of paper. "We have an operation up-island. We aren't sure exactly where. But someone came into the northern detachment office in Nanaimo and gave a statement to the officer on duty. This guy, aged nineteen, has been working for an operation near Union Bay. He gets picked up at his house in Cumberland on Sunday, there are usually three of four other guys in the van not counting the driver. They're taken somewhere in the dark, he doesn't know where. They end up in a tunnel or a dark shed or something. They work there for four days, doing long hours, bunking in a side room, and then are driven home Thursday night. So again, they can't see where they are. They're paid for their work in cash. And the wages are considerable."

"Hmm." Rain wondered what his role would be in this scenario, but big wages sounded like some high-end activity.

"Yeah, hmm," said Ross. "Our guy up there says there are a number of young men without jobs in the Cumberland area who live rather well—new vehicles, which is where most young guys put their money, trips to Mexico, and so on."

"New vehicles?" said Rain. "That's stupid. A new car or truck loses about a third of its value in the first couple of years. And there's nothing to attract attention faster than a flashy car. It's like waving a red flag. I should know."

Ross had been the lead police detective on Rain's case and had worked hard for months to track him down. Now he sat back and levelled a look at him. "You always drove beaters."

"Yeah, except they weren't."

"No, they just looked like it, but they ran well," Ross acknowledged reluctantly, running his fingers through his close-cropped dark hair.

"Right." Rain shrugged. "No use buying a vehicle that doesn't do the job. I had a good mechanic who kept an eye out for me. He'd buy something that looked rough and needed work. Then he'd fix it up and I'd trade in my old one."

"Hmm. Well that's not the story here apparently." Ross

glanced back at the page, following his finger down the lines of writing. "There are also signs of a new source of drugs in the area. Comox, Cumberland, Nanaimo, etc. With the military base in Comox, the police—both civilian and military- keep a keen eye out for that sort of stuff. They've noticed a river of meth coming through."

"Okay," said Rain. "That's not good."

"No, it's not. but they can't locate the source. I'm thinking that if we can find the money, we can trace it back to whoever is running this operation."

"I see. My experience is quite different from this story." Rain tugged on his lower lip.

Irritably, Ross closed the file folder and tossed it across the desk toward him. "Use your imagination," he barked. "We don't seem to be getting anywhere, maybe you can."

Rain straightened in his chair, gripping the folder with one hand. This wasn't the first case that he'd worked on with the cops, but he hoped it would be his last. In the past months, each time they gave him a file to work, he'd been able to contribute some insight that the police sources had missed. It was rewarding to be able to provide some useful information. At the same time, he'd had enough. He was tired of being pulled in so many directions, getting his orders to appear here, go there, do this or that, all on someone else's timeline. He was ready to resume his own life, get his affairs back under his control and direction— make his own decisions.

He turned to Ross Cullen "I need a new identity," he said. "I don't want to use my own name for a job like this. When I'm finished with the case, I need to go back to being

Rainier Murdoch. I don't want to worry that someone might come looking for me."

"Okay." Ross shoved his chair back and got to his feet. "I can make that happen."

***

CHAPTER FOUR

Rain pulled his truck to the curb in front of the federal building on Vancouver Street and parked. Climbing out, he fished in his pocket for some coins to feed the meter. Here he was again, keeping his weekly appointment with the probation officer. This had been going on for months, an irritating part of his probation conditions. The guy was okay to deal with, though he seemed a bit preoccupied, loaded up with paperwork, and had little interest in what Rain had to say. It was just part of the arrangement— make contact weekly. Rain entered and grabbed a chair in the featureless waiting room. The receptionist gave him a sympathetic look and said, "Nigel's running a little behind."

"No problem," he replied and checked his phone. A message from Ross Cullen recommending Rain come by his office this afternoon. Ross had his new ID ready and more information on the case. Good, that might be helpful. Rain had planned to head up-island tomorrow and the ID would be some protection from whatever he might encounter in his explorations. More information would be good too. The added details would make it safer and easier for him to find out what was going on. He'd like to interview the boy who'd given his statement to the police. He wanted to get his own take on what the guy knew and why he'd given evidence. Was he afraid? Did he feel trapped in the cycle of work? And what kind of work did they do in the dark shed or tunnel? Why hadn't the police pried that information out of him? When the opportunity presented itself, they should have taken full advantage of it.

He took a small notebook out of his breast pocket and made a few notations on the first page — items to remind himself what he was looking for, then tucked it away again. He was starting to feel like a cop. He glanced around the room at the small group of seemingly disinterested men, all here waiting to see their probation officer. Most of them were staring at their boots in resignation.

Then a guy noisily stalked down the hall and out the front door, a thunderous expression on his face. The receptionist picked up the phone and murmured something. She set it back in the cradle and waved at Rain. "He'll see you now, Mr. Murdoch."

"Great. Thank you." He stood, just as Nigel appeared in the hallway to show him through. Rain walked forward, his hand held out in greeting. "Hi, Nigel."

The officer stared at him a moment as his own hand slowly rose. "Hi Rainier," he said, giving him a firm shake. "Good to see you. Come on back." He turned and led the way to his tiny office.

Rain took a seat and examined the file on the desktop, looking for some indication it was his document. "Anything new?" he asked.

"Not sure. Give me a minute." Nigel flipped the top file closed and grabbed another from the array on his desk. "I've made application to put you on a new schedule. I don't see any reason for you to call in here every week. I've got lots of guys who need way more attention than you do."

Something eased in Rain's gut. "Yeah, that would be easier to manage. I don't have much time left on my probation order anyway, and I'm supposed to go up-island tomorrow. Not sure when I'll be back."

Nigel looked alarmed. "Why are you leaving town?"

"Police work. Part of the terms of my probation." Rain clamped his lips together.

"Oh, okay, sure. I think you're the only guy I have on my roster who works with the police. You caught me off guard there." The probation officer glanced down at the file again. "Yeah, here's the approval from the judge. So, once a month will be enough, I figure. Thanks for dropping by and see you again next month. If you can't make it in to see me, here's my card. Give me a call. Either way, I expect to hear from you."

"Perfect." Rain stood and extended his hand again. "Thanks, Nigel. I'll be in touch."

Nigel took his hand and gripped it warmly. "You do that," he said.

~~~

Rain's stop at the RCMP detachment was just as productive. Ross was out of the office, but a couple of envelopes had been left for Rain at the reception desk on the main floor. There was a credit card inside the first one, along with his new driver's licence. The picture on the licence looked good and his name was now Dexter Winston. *Was this a joke?* Who called their child Dexter? When he was choosing his own aliases, years ago, he'd stuck to real identification, so his names had been things like Tom or Bob, easy to remember and easy for others to forget. The good news was, he wasn't likely to forget this name. When someone said *Dexter*, it would certainly catch his attention.

He sighed, tucked the new cards into his pocket and opened the other envelope. A business card for a police officer at the Nanaimo RCMP detachment and the printout of a photo of a man who was still young enough to have pimples on his chin along with a copy of the guy's statement to police. No name for the informant, however. More information to work with, for sure. With the help of the cops, he'd be able to find this guy once he reached Cumberland. Then he could ask his own questions.

***

CHAPTER FIVE

Ross Cullen drove toward home. His workday had been interesting, particularly regarding his time with Rainier Murdoch. Ross had been the lead detective on Murdoch's case years ago, and it was his dogged determination and hard work that had finally gotten the man arrested, after months of searching for leads and following red herrings. Murdoch was one bright man, he'd give him that. But he'd made a few mistakes in the course of his flight, and Ross picked up on some of them, capturing him at last. Now he was on probation.

He smiled in satisfaction and shifted into third gear for the climb on the south road out of town. Murdoch had a business partner, a man named Jeff Sanderson, who had disappeared. That's when Ross had met Sanderson's wife, Chloe Bowman, and fallen in love. He remembered the stress of those days, longing for a woman whose husband was a criminal and had vanished without a trace. At that point, he'd probably been close to losing his job from his own preoccupations.

He gulped some air and backed off his speed. Now he was

married to Sanderson's widow. She was the joy of his life and Rainier Murdoch was her business partner. She had inherited her husband's business interests, which had been held jointly by Sanderson and Murdoch.

He pulled into the drive and pushed a button to lift the garage door, eased his car into his space, and turned off the engine. Chloe's car was already there. The door to the house opened and a little boy appeared, a huge grin on his face as he bobbed up and down on his toes in excitement.

"Davey," he called, and the boy beetled across the concrete to leap into his arms. "How are you, little guy?"

"Fine," said Davey, his face turning sober. "I'm glad you're home." He loved questions and always did his best to tell the whole truth. "Mum is making cookies."

Ross raised his brows in fake astonishment. "She is? Wow!"

The boy nodded. "Yeah, wow. She's the best cook, and they've got chocolate chips in them, too."

"Oh, man. I love that kind." He squeezed Davey against his chest. "Don't you?"

"Yup. They're my favourite."

"Me too." He stepped through the doorway into the hall and set him down. "Wonder what's for dinner?"

Davey shook his head. "Don't know." He wasn't as interested in his dinner, obviously.

He raced ahead of Ross, disappearing into the kitchen. "Mummy, Dad's here." Ross felt his heart roll over in his chest. He was so lucky. Davey had accepted him into the family, even before he married Chloe, and started calling him Dad right away. It was a gift. And now with Amy, their daughter of seven months, his life was full. Never did he imagine as a single man what it would be like to be married to the woman he loved and have two children, a family. He marvelled at the reality of it every day.

Chloe peeked around the corner, a mischievous look on her face. "I figured you were here," she said. "Davey was watching the drive and then raced down the hall to the garage. I couldn't think what else it could mean."

He looked into her dear face, beautiful pale skin surrounded by wavy black hair, just like Snow White. His chest clenched. "Brat," he said, and leaned forward to plant a firm kiss on her mouth, carefully avoiding her hands holding spoons with dough clinging to them. The sense of possessiveness and belonging was instantaneous.

"Look out," she said, pulling back. "Amy's on the floor trying to travel and she's getting around pretty fast using the GI Joe jungle crawl." She stuck the spoons into the bowl of dough just as the oven timer dinged. "Can you find her while I get this?"

Davey waved at them from over near the kitchen table. "She's right here! She crawled all the way from the doorway." He got down on his knees and patted her back while the baby chortled up at him.

Ross walked over and picked the baby up, giving her a smacking kiss on her red cheek. While Davey looked like his mother, with the pale skin and black wavy hair, the little girl had inherited his darker skin. The red cheeks told how much effort and excitement had gone into the crawling exercise.

"Good boy, Davey, for looking after her. You're the best big brother." As the boy gave him a cheeky grin, so like his mother's, he turned back to Chloe. "I had an interesting meeting with your business partner today." He pulled Amy's fingers out of his mouth.

'Oh, good." She took a pan from the oven and slid another one in. "How is he? I haven't spoken to him in a while."

"He's anxious to get off probation."

She gave him a reproving look. "Of course he is. It must be soon now."

"Yup. This is his last case."

"Case?" She removed the cookies from the pan with a spatula, then began plopping more chunks of dough on it in a steady rhythm.

"I've got him working on an investigation for me. We weren't getting anywhere with it, so I thought I'd put him on it. He's one smart man."

"Yes, he is." She looked pensive.

Ross moved closer and pulled her into his free arm. "I'm not casting aspersions on your ex," he said.

"I know. But working with Rainier has been interesting. He's generous-hearted, you know? As well as being really bright. I find him very supportive in all the decisions I make about the building. It's seldom he questions what I do, and if he does, it's because he has come up with a better idea. Kind of intimidating, really."

"Don't worry, you're every bit as clever as he is." He kissed her temple and tried to extract the clump of her hair the baby had grabbed in her sticky elastic fingers.

By the time he succeeded, Chloe had dropped her spoons and Davey had come over to help. Ross gathered them all into his arms and hugged them tight. His own family.

***

CHAPTER SIX

During the busy day preparing for a trip up-island, Rain texted Sophia. He felt compelled to see her before he disappeared to Nanaimo or further north. It had been a while since he'd spent time with a woman, having been a year on the run before he was arrested. But his long-time girlfriend Trudy Ashmore had gotten hooked on drugs. Back then he'd been ready to pop the question, marry and settle down to start a family. Thinking about it now, he realized living undercover was not the ideal position to be in when entering a serious relationship, and her addiction to drugs had put paid to that idea, anyway.

Too late. This new investigation with Detective Cullen might just nip any new plans he had in the bud. It was starting to look like he'd be back undercover. He fingered the official *Dexter Winston* ID in his pocket. Was he actually contemplating getting serious with Sophia? He'd just encountered her, for the first time in years. He shoved the idea aside, in no position to get serious with anyone. Yet she was almost family. He couldn't pretend she didn't matter.

Are you still up for dinner? he texted

Yes, perfect, Sophia replied.

They connected at the Indian Cuisine Restaurant on the road leading out of town in the direction of Uncle Toby's house. Apparently, she was still staying out there, hopefully by herself, although he hunched his shoulders at that thought.

Rain drove his truck into the parking lot and waited as light rain spattered on his windshield. He was a few minutes early. If he saw her entering the lot, he'd find out what she was driving and be able to escort her into the place. Two birds with one stone. He gave an ironic grin just as a brand new grey Audi maneuvered around the corner and into a parking spot near the front door of the restaurant. It was a V-8 model, he could hear the rumble of the engine from inside the cab of his truck. The black convertible top was a highly noticeable detail.

Thea Sophia unsnapped her seatbelt and climbed out of the vehicle, slamming the door. She was wearing a pretty honey-coloured blouse with deep cleavage that gave him a good view of the tops of her breasts. A pair of khaki shorts showcased her shapely legs. Little black sandals with sparkly beads on them covered her feet. The sight immediately started his heart pounding a little faster.

The car she drove wasn't flashy but it was good quality. Expensive, too. He pondered the income required to finance such a purchase. Did she have a boyfriend who paid for things like cars? He'd better find out before he got too involved with her.

There was that thought again, the startling idea that he

might be considering getting involved, after only one meeting out at Toby's house. Well, they had a history, he and Thea Sophia. Growing up, Sophia had always been in his face, demanding his attention, right up until he graduated from high school and left the farm to come to Victoria for university.

But at the moment he had questions. If she was staying at her father's house, she had abandoned any job that would contribute to her lifestyle, including making car payments. How did she survive?

He opened his door. "Sophia," he called as he stepped out into the mist. She startled and turned toward him, her face set and pale. Then she smiled, a tiny dimple appearing at the corner of her mouth. There was a jolt in his chest. He remembered that dimple. "Wait up," he said, jogging toward her.

He took her hand. It felt small and soft in his as he led her toward the steps. "Have you eaten here before?" he asked. "The food's pretty good but you have to like pakoras and samosas, it's spicy."

She laughed, a tinkling sound that slithered down his spine. "Can't wait," she replied. "There's nothing like this up-Island."

He froze. "How do you mean, up-island? Are you going away?"

She slanted a glance at him as he opened the door. "No, but I was living up there. This is a nice change."

He gazed at her face, large pale blue eyes outlined with long thick lashes, short straight nose and full lips, the tiny dimple at the corner. He needed to keep his head on straight. He was going up-Island on an investigation, and she used to live up there. The investigation involved money laundering, and she was driving a sleek expensive new car, yet had no visible means of support. "Put on your thinking cap, Rainier," as Dad always used to say. Rain didn't see Dad all that much these days. Moose Jaw wasn't on his personal trajectory when he had to stay in Victoria to report to probation weekly or answer Ross Cullen's summons, whenever they arrived, to aid in a police investigation.

"We have a reservation," Rain said to the greeter in the entry, and they were led to a quiet table in the corner. If for any reason he needed to show his ID, all he had to remember was to pull out the one that said *Murdoch*.

***

CHAPTER SEVEN

Sophia folded a napkin in her lap and gave him an accusatory glare. "I haven't seen much of you, Rainier Murdoch. Not since you left the farm."

"I've been home a few times, but Toby had already sold your land," he shot back, acknowledging her jab. A big enterprise started buying up the farmsteads around them, their giant equipment designed to handle and farm many more acres of land than a single family ever could. The remaining farmers were resentful and bitter about the lifestyle changes forced upon them by the new competition. Rain remembered many heated conversations with his father about that very issue. Dad felt betrayed by Toby's move off the land.

"Yes, we got a house in the city of Moose Jaw. Dad had signed up with the Royal Canadian Mounted Police by then, he worked out of that detachment office."

"I'm sure you saw enough of me to last a lifetime after your mother died," he said. The whole family of Bonnar children had moved in with the Murdoch's at their farm. They'd taken the same school bus together every morning.

She smiled. "That was so kind of your folks to take us in. All but my brother, Toby. He stayed with Dad to work on the farm."

"Right." Rain moved his fork an inch to the left. "Tough times. Your younger sister and brothers used to cry themselves to sleep every night. It was heartbreaking to see."

"I know. Your Mum stepped in and mothered us all." She glanced down and sat back as the waiter brought the food to their table.

"Yeah. Mum's like that. She's got her arms around everyone."

"I still love her like she was my own mother," she said.

Rain focussed on her face. "How old were you when your mum died?"

"Fourteen. Toby was sixteen and thought he was an adult, kind of quit school and worked the farm."

"Until your father sold the land. That must have been quite a shock for him. You know, after that he used to come out at harvest time and work with Dad on the combine." He squinted as he thought about it. "Jake and I were both there, but he came anyway. With four guys it really moved things along."

"I know. He still does that, loves the farm work." Sophia took a bite of samosa and her eyes watered. She panted with her mouth open and waved a hand in front of her face. "Wow, you did say it would be spicy."

Rain grinned and forked a bite into his mouth. "It's great. Keeps the blood vessels working fine."

"When we first moved in with your family, you had to give up your room." Sophia wiped a tear from her cheek and fixed her gaze on his face.

He gave a short nod. "True. We needed to free up a bedroom for you kids and mine was bigger than Jake's."

"Is that why?" She looked at him doubtfully. "At night when your mother put the kids to bed, you used to go up with them."

"What do you mean?" He used his fork to cut another bite from his samosa.

"I mean they would all cry if they were left alone in the room. Lots of times I saw you sitting on the floor, telling them stories." She blinked rapidly, her eyes shining with tears. He didn't know if it was emotion or the spicy food, although she hadn't tried another bite.

"Leah didn't cry," he replied self-consciously.

"That was because you held her hand while you talked. They all listened, Ted in bed beside Leah, Pete and Randy in the other bed, both sucking their thumbs."

"Pete had stopped sucking his thumb by then," Rain protested. "He was five."

"Yeah," she replied. "but after Mum died, he went back to it. It was a comfort for him."

"Poor little tykes," he muttered.

"Yes, and you decided it was your job to comfort them. Why Rain?"

He bristled. "What do you mean, why? Anyone would have

done the same if they could. Besides, I made up a great story, I still think about it sometimes and add chapters in my head." He grinned, hoping to distract her from the topic.

"I've never been able to find out what story you told them. None of them would divulge the details." She gave him an inquisitive look.

"That's because it's top secret. We had all sworn to never tell, and those kids respected that."

He thought about Ted, Pete and Randy and how little they'd been in those days. Leah wasn't much older but had more composure somehow. Is that how it worked—boys took longer to grow up? Perhaps. In the end, the kids had all moved back home with Sophia in the role of mother, running the household for her father while he went off to work.

"I'm sorry about Pete. I couldn't get home for the funeral. The police were still after me."

A tear tracked down her cheek as she tried to smile. "That's okay. Although most people have a better excuse for not showing up at an event like that."

"I know," he replied, his gaze following the tear down her cheek until she brushed it away. "Not something I'm proud of." He paused. "He died in a fight on the streets at night, right?"

"Yes, but they told us he was high on meth. I didn't even know he used the stuff."

Her expression broke his heart. "It's not your fault, Sophia. You couldn't have stopped him from getting involved with whatever he was hooked on. No one could."

33

She glanced down and fiddled with her knife. "In my head, I know that. But in my heart…"

Rain lifted his shoulders in an awkward shrug. "I know. The older sibling feels responsible for the younger ones. Even though you aren't, and never could be. His father was in the police, for heaven's sake, and that didn't stop him."

They sat in silence for a moment. Sophia took another bite of her pakora, followed with a sip from her glass of wine.

"How old were you when you all moved back home?" he asked.

"I was sixteen," she said. "After that we left the farm, so it was a lot less work. In the city we had running water instead of a well. Central heating in our apartment instead of hauling in firewood, a bus that ran right down our street."

Rain laughed and laid his hand palm up on the table. Cautiously she put her hand in his and he closed his fingers around it. Something eased in his chest. It felt absolutely perfect. It felt right. "Staying at your father's house now is a far cry from the farm. I guess you can see why he bought it."

She smiled, the tiny dimple appearing and disappearing. Rain knew he was falling fast and should put the brakes on if he could. He didn't have the whole story about Thea Sophia, and it made him uncomfortable.

He removed his hand and went back to his dinner, noting the disappointment on her face. It was reflected in his chest.

***

CHAPTER EIGHT

Thea Sophia drove down the dark and winding country road toward her father's house. She called herself Sophia now, Thea Sophia was her mother. Rainier lived in town, so he'd exited the restaurant parking lot after her, heading in the other direction.

Headlights appeared in her rear-view mirror, approaching swiftly and causing her to tense, her heart speeding in alarm. Soon they lit up the whole interior of her car and she pressed hard on the gas pedal to avoid being hit from behind, muscles tight in her chest. Now she was going faster than was comfortable on a still unfamiliar road, but the vehicle was coming up on her so quickly it seemed it might rear-end her car. Then the lights slowed and the car turned off onto a side road. Her shoulders relaxed. She could take a breath and get home in a better frame of mind.

The idea that Anton might still be looking for her kept her stomach in a knot. Many months ago, before she made the decision to leave him, their relationship had disintegrated into something she didn't recognize—he was angry and demanding, physically threatening and sometimes violent. She didn't know what she'd done wrong but the bruises on her arms and chest were proof things weren't going well. If she'd gone to Dad's immediately after leaving, Anton would have followed within hours. So she'd played a decoy game, taking the ferry off the Island, leaving from Nanaimo to Vancouver early one morning just after Anton went to work so he wouldn't be aware until evening that she had left him. The ploy had given her a head start and some breathing room.

She didn't trust him for a minute, with all his talk of surveillance and tracking, so she'd taken her car to a garage in Burnaby on the mainland and asked them to search for anything that might alert someone to her location. The technician had found a tracking device under the front bumper, glued in place. He'd drilled it off and smashed it, throwing the debris in the garbage can. "You've got a determined man on your tail," he quipped, giving her body the once over with his pointed gaze.

"It's not anything I'd wish on your sister," she replied, and his expression quickly changed to one of alarm and protection.

"Let me have another look," he said and used his wand on the interior of her car. He found another device under the rear bumper and a signal under the back seat, a device clamped to the springs. "It's pretty weak," he explained, "but we'll remove it anyway."

Staying at a low-cost hotel, she'd contemplated her next moves. This was not a strategy that had just occurred to her. She'd known for a long time she'd have to leave. She didn't want to go across the American border from here, even though she'd brought her passport with her. Anton Ganaye was a cop and he could access government records too easily. He'd know where she'd gone and how to manage the search to find her. Her car was a dead give away, but there was little she could do about that at the moment. She couldn't sell or trade it without alerting him, because he'd registered a lien against it, even though nothing was owed. Anton knew how to keep her close, and under his control.

The car was her biggest issue because it was such a noticeable vehicle, and Anton could always put out a traffic alert for her licence plate. He'd soon know where she was. "The cops look after their own," was his favourite expression. She should park it in Dad's garage and drive his old truck. She just hadn't found his keys. Maybe he took them with him. Her next task was to text Dad and find out where he kept the truck keys. She worried Anton was monitoring her phone. She needed to get a new one with a different number. So much to do, so little energy.

It had been good to spend time with Rainier. She and Rain's younger brother, Jake Murdoch, had been in the same grade going through school. Jake was cute, and idolized his older brother. Rain had hardly been around to help out on the farm except in planting and harvest season. He'd been a member of the debating team for the grad year, played hockey for their school, and worked a night job at the local movie theatre. He had his own vehicle back then, which he'd bought with his own money, Jake reported with pride. It was a battered old pickup with a club cab so he could ferry his buddies around.

She'd always been fascinated by Rainier, or Rain Man as his friends called him. She hadn't understood the nickname then, but had since seen the movie, *Rain Man*, with the actor Dustin Hoffman in the lead role, and realized it was a reference to Rain's great brain and memory for detail.

Her phone chirped and she pulled it from her purse. A text from Rain—*Call me when you get home.*

Okay, she thumbed.

What was he doing, looking after the Bonnars again? Did that mean anything when it came to her specifically, or was it just his reflex reaction with her family? She'd be foolish to read too much into it. She didn't need to have her heart stomped on all over again.

***

CHAPTER NINE

Sophia rolled over in bed. She'd set the alarm at the front door before getting ready to retire. She knew how it worked, even if Rain liked to tease and pretend otherwise. It was a comfort to know a loud noise would wake her if someone were to break into the house or open any of the exterior doors while she was sleeping. A signal would also go to the alarm company, and Dad had explained they would call the police before calling the house to check on her.

She peered at the bedroom windows where the blinds had been lowered. No light showed around them. There were no streetlights here, she was too far out of the city center. Her car was safely stowed in the garage, so it wasn't sitting in the drive like a red flag, or a *grey* flag, to alert anyone to her whereabouts. She smiled against the pillow. If only she could find the keys to Dad's truck, things would be much more comfortable.

She hadn't texted him, confident Anton would be tracking the activity on her phone through police systems, even though she had turned off the feature that reported her current location.

She'd opened a new bank account the other day, depositing all the money she'd withdrawn in cash from the old one. She didn't want to leave a trail. At the same time, she ordered a new credit card, now that she had a job that would bring in some money. She hadn't been actively looking for work, but Dad knew someone who knew someone, and she'd been volunteered for this position which seemed to be exactly what she needed. She'd meet people and make a little money.

She didn't mind the work—it was interesting and might even help her in this conflict with Anton. Plus, it provided the backing she needed for a new bank account and credit card.

She relaxed into the warm sheets. Talking to Rain brought back a lot of memories. After Mum died and the Bonnar children had moved in with the Murdochs on the next farm, she'd been jealous of her younger siblings, having Rainier there every night to talk to them, tell stories and reassure their fears.

She'd been sleeping in the spare bed in Susan's room. Susan was older than Rain and didn't seem as approachable. So Sophia had scrunched down in the blankets every night, feeling like crying, but afraid to look foolish. She wasn't three or six like the little ones. Yet they had someone to cuddle with when they went to sleep, after Rain soothed them with his stories. She had been alone in her bed.

Just like now. She didn't miss Anton that way. He'd worked a lot of nights and wasn't an emotional man, didn't show his feelings, at least not to her. They'd met in a Moose Jaw bar, and after a few dates he'd convinced her to move to

Vancouver Island. He was police and had a big promotion on the horizon that involved working undercover in western Canada.

There wasn't much holding her in Saskatchewan. Dad had already left, been transferred in the police force, her brother Toby was doing his best to buy a farm, and her younger siblings hung around in a pack that didn't include her.

She'd moved west, though not her best decision, now that she thought about it. She'd dropped her university courses mid-term and gone with Anton Ganaye. Except that's not how it had been. Anton didn't have his own residence, at the time he was bunking with friends, but he promised things would be better in Comox, British Columbia—a place she'd never heard of.

They did have a decent house to live in there, a three-bedroom bungalow that she occupied primarily alone. Anton worked long hours, often at night, always out of town. He spent a lot of time commuting to and from work and never talked about his job. Everything he did as an undercover cop was totally confidential, he reminded her constantly.

Here she was with history repeating itself, living alone in a big house. Alone and afraid. For once in her life, Rainier seemed to be taking notice instead of ignoring her. But was she hoping to hook up with Rainier Murdoch, just as he took on a job working undercover for the police? Everything was going to be confidential.

Would she never learn?

***

CHAPTER TEN

It was early evening, dusk just falling when Kofi Aribadis left his basement suite carrying a duffel bag containing everything he would need for the following week at work. He tossed it in the trunk of his car and climbed into the driver's seat. The second-hand Mercedes Benz wasn't something he could have afforded for himself, but it was a job perc so he couldn't complain. It didn't cost him anything but the gas to drive it.

His landlord thought it humourous that he lived in the basement of his rental house in Union Bay and sublet the main floor to a small family. But Kofi hadn't come to Canada to live the high life. He came to make a new life, which was much different. The basement suite suited him just fine, living alone as he did, and saved him a lot of money.

When he first arrived in North America, he'd crossed over the Canadian border from the United States and was immediately arrested and put into immigrant housing. But that wasn't his goal—to live off government programmes until he was deported back to Ethiopia. He had family back home that required his support, a wife and children who he hoped would arrive soon to keep him company. He missed them all dearly. His father was not well, and had trouble getting the heart medicine he needed to thrive. Mother was worried about her husband, but also about her eldest son living alone in a foreign country.

Kofi sent emails daily, reassuring them of his safety, and the wonderful place where he lived. At home, they made the trip to the library to read his missives and send back the news from their end. He was on the exact other side of the earth, but it was hard for them to grasp that fact. There weren't any countries near Ethiopia the size of Canada. The fact he'd travelled all the way to the eastern United States was a mind-boggling idea for them. They had no concept of the size of Canada and how far away the west coast was from the east coast of Africa.

Nor did he tell them about the struggle of trying to find a job when he looked so different from the average person he met in this country. After arrival, he'd sent out numerous work applications, with no good results. Then he'd met Anton Ganaye. Anton said he was a cop and had a job for him that would pay in cash. Given that payment in cash was the usual method back home, Kofi hadn't been taken aback, although the idea of dealing with the police could be alarming. Ganaye had dark skin too, not as dark as Kofi's, but not like most of the whities he worked with. That was one reason he'd decided to trust this offer. He'd been desperate to get going on his family's plan.

Aribadis started his car. The deep purring rumble of the engine under the hood was reassuring. He'd never come across a vehicle like this back home. When he said 'go' this car went, no hesitation. Getting his driver's licence here had been a bit of a challenge but he took some lessons and managed to pass the test, barely. Language was the real problem. Kofi could read and write. He'd spent two or three years in school back home and he even spoke English as well as Oromo and Arabic. But English was different here—the sound of a word did not match the look of it on paper. Three years later, it still remained a challenge for him.

The sooner he could get his children here, the better. Children learned at a faster rate than adults, and the question of learning English would be easier for them to handle while young. Plus he had high hopes of more children—three youngsters was not a big family in Ethiopia.

Anton Ganaye ran his life now. Aribadis often wished he'd managed to land a different job before he ran into Ganaye. Yes, he had work. Yes, he was paid in cash and it was certainly enough to run his life here and ship some money home to his family. His oldest son was smart. With the first payment home, he'd bought himself a cell phone. Now Kofi could send money directly to his wife and kids via the phone as well as text them short messages. He still saved the longer letters for email, and he treasured the ones he received in return.

But after some months of work, he'd overheard enough discussions and arguments between Anton and his partner, Leon, to understand the work he did was not legal work. The stuff they produced was not legal product. There were reasons why the plant was run the way it was—the workers coming in at night, staying for four days and leaving at night. The plant was well hidden. Even when Kofi drove to work, he hid his car inside the cavern where the plant was located and all the activity took place.

A man in a foreign country on a work permit shouldn't be doing this kind of work. His ability to stay in the country would be at risk if he were ever arrested. And he'd discovered Anton was no cop. He had nothing to offer in the way of protection when the real police stepped in.

Aribadis stopped at the gate to the plant. He blinked his headlights and waited for Gerra to roll up the camouflage curtain and let him enter. He was always punctual. He knew Gerra would be leaving in ten minutes to pick up the workers. He pulled his car to the side and stepped out. As usual the dogs surrounded him, barking, sniffing at his legs and licking his shoes. He waved them off as Gerra ordered them back to their kennels.

Grabbing his clipboard, he began checking supplies for this new batch of product, ticking off the items as he counted. Anton had his sources and kept the plant well stocked for most of the materials needed. The propane tank was getting low. He made a note to call Anton. He had a special supplier who delivered directly and filled it for a cash payment.

The other issue was garbage. Aribadis had been given the task of taking care of the waste generated by the plant. He had tried to get Gerra to take care of some of it, but the Mexican had baulked at the idea. Gerra was wary of doing anything to attract the wrong kind of attention. In addition, he had his own orders from Ganaye, and the garbage wasn't his problem. Thus, Kofi made a trip up or down island every week. He bundled the garbage and travelled a different road each time, tossing the bags out the window. He had a map on which he'd numbered the byways leading out of Union Bay and travelled them one by one so a pattern was undiscernible by whoever might be looking. He didn't want his life plan to be knocked off track because of garbage. He'd also noted commercial dumpsters in shopping malls in the area and took advantage of those when there was no one around to notice.

Next he began a list of food supplies. He'd been hearing complaints from the workers about the quality of their meals, and with men this age, quantity was always an issue as well. You'd think they spent all day digging a field for planting, they way they scarfed down everything in sight that was edible. Best to be ready. Nothing produced a cranky group of workers as fast as hunger. Not that these boys knew the meaning of the word. Due to the ongoing civil war back home, Kofi knew lots of young men who could explain from their own personal experience what it meant to be hungry.

***

CHAPTER ELEVEN

Rain stopped in to see Detective Ross Cullen one more time. Cullen didn't have any information to add to what he'd already provided, but he handed over a cell phone for Rain's use. "Reception is sketchy in some of those little towns," he warned. "This should provide the coverage you'll need. It's on the police network. Be careful. The communities are small. Everyone knows everyone. You'll stand out from the crowd the minute you show up and start asking questions."

"Right, got it," Rain replied. "I'll let you know where I am and where I'm staying."

"Okay." Ross nodded. "I'll share that with Detective Vickers, the detachment officer up there who's spearheading the case."

"I see," Rain paused. "So, I should go and meet him first. I want to talk to the young man who gave the information anyway. I've got more questions."

"I doubt they'll let you contact him. Too dangerous. But you can give it a try."

"Well," Rain grumbled, "I hope the police up there cooperate with me, or I won't get anywhere fast."

Ross shrugged. "Let me know if you have any problems. Sometimes cops don't like to work with a civilian, you know? I can be your reference."

"Good." Rain left the small cubicle, taking a deep breath. *Here we go*, he thought. *I hope I can provide some benefit to this investigation. I need to finish probation.* After this case closed, the end was in sight. He'd be free.

His patience was wearing thin. He wanted to pursue his own goals, find out what the story was on Sophia, discover if she was seeing anyone.

It didn't take long to reach Cumberland. On the drive north Rain puzzled over what he had learned about Thea Sophia Bonnar. When he'd called her name in the parking lot at the restaurant, she'd startled and her face had gone white with alarm. It was apparent even in the gloom of the evening she was nervous. What was she running from? Or more likely, who? He just didn't know, but he was pretty sure she was concealing something. Maybe the guy who paid for the car might be of interest, if indeed it was a guy. He'd almost asked her outright last night, but lost his nerve. Perhaps he didn't want to know.

The fact was, if he didn't sort it out, he couldn't date her. No way was he getting involved with a woman who was already involved, so to speak. He had principles, even if it didn't look like it from the outside. Pulling to the side of the road, he took out the little notebook from his pocket. *Owner search on Sophia's car*, he wrote, adding the licence plate number from the photo he'd taken of it that night at the restaurant. Might as well get what info he could. The police search system was available and at his fingertips.

When he reached it, Cumberland looked like an old company town. There were quite a few of these on Vancouver Island, he had discovered. Most of the Island had been settled by companies that were focussed on the abundant natural resources to be found here. A few of the establishments were fishing villages along the coast, where long docks lined with fishing boats stretched out into the water of a sheltered bay. Others had been built to house families of loggers who worked in the forestry industry. Some, like this town, had been built to service the families of miners who worked in the various active mines.

They all shared a similar layout—two-story houses with three or four bedrooms, situated close together along narrow streets. There was usually a church, a school, a dam to provide clean community water, and a small commercial area housing a grocery store and a gas station. Company towns ensured the working staff could live close enough to report for duty every day. Rain didn't know the whole history of Cumberland, but he was aware there had been quite a number of coal mines in the area, all now closed.

He cruised through the village and what he saw confirmed the comments from Ross. It was small. He could tell that even having the same new vehicle drive through the narrow streets once too often would raise concerns among the residents.

The difficulty would be to hang around long enough to learn what he needed to know without sounding an alarm.

He would be looking for someone with money to burn—a flashy vehicle, designer clothes, spending money like water. On the other hand, the fastest way to find out about the work would be to park on the edge of town and locate the van that ferried the workers out and back. Then follow the van. Why hadn't the cops already done that?

How did these three or four young men manage to do their work under the radar, while being picked up and dropped off each week? One of the residents would know something. In a village this size that was always the case. He just had to find the person who was willing to talk.

***

CHAPTER TWELVE

Anton Ganaye clicked his signal on and steered his pickup into the right-hand travelling lane of the northbound highway. The vehicle behind him had been too close to his tailgate for comfort and he was sure it was an undercover cop car. The crash bars on the front grill and the large side mirrors were dead giveaways. He cruised just below the speed limit, hoping the guy would pass him and disappear. Instead, the other driver signalled and pulled into the travelling lane behind him, still riding his tail.

Anton had spent the night in Nanaimo unloading the latest pack of product from the plant and was heading back to Union Bay to check on progress there. He was antsy about the way things were going. Where was Sophia? She'd been gone for months and he missed her. He was also concerned about what she might know. It was frustrating as hell that he hadn't been able to find her after she left. He'd watched for her car, knowing she must have run out of cash by now. He was pretty sure she didn't know about his business endeavours, but she knew him. The last thing he needed was a wildcard woman on the loose with a hate-on for him. Who knew what she'd do or who she'd talk to? Her father was a cop, and although they didn't seem to be close, Mr Bonnar lived on Vancouver Island, on the outskirts of Victoria. If she went there, the father would want to know what had happened, what he'd done to her.

Anton glanced in the rear-view mirror and cursed under his breath. What was this cop's problem? The insurance on the truck was current, thus the requisite little tag glued to his licence plate. The guy had probably already checked that. Anton wasn't speeding but the cab of his truck was loaded with supplies for the plant. His shoulders tensed as he prepared for the siren. Then he spied the turn off on the righthand side of the highway that led into the village of Lantzville. He flicked on his signal and slowed even more, easing into the off lane. In his side mirror, he watched the cop car cruise on past as he escaped down the ramp.

At last, he was free. No need to rush. He'd stop for a coffee before he went back onto the highway. A few minutes later, he sat in his truck nursing a hot cup. When a guy lived covert like he did, it was always better to stay out of the public eye. He'd check his equipment when he got home tonight for any further information on her Audi. But shortly after Sophia left, the trackers in her car stopped functioning. How did that happen? One tracker could have fallen off, but it was unlikely they all had. And at the same time? Not believable.

The last information showed her car in Vancouver on the mainland, but he had no idea where she might have gone since. She could have carried on down into Washington State, or headed back home to the Prairies in Saskatchewan. Maybe he wouldn't be able to find her after all. It was a startling idea and not one he entertained willingly. He missed having her around, his bed was empty and cold.

Time to invest more resources in the effort to locate her. He'd been distracted with all the upheaval at the plant. His focus was off the search. If nothing else, he wanted the car back. That had been a very expensive purchase and he wasn't getting any benefit from it now, was he?

After his stop in Union Bay, he'd go straight home. There was a lot to do.

~~~

Sitting at his kitchen table, Anton read his list again.

Find new workers for the plant—should be easy. Cumberland was a pretty desolate place with few employment opportunities for young men that paid what he paid.

Ensure Aribadis was onside—he needed surveillance equipment in there. Aribadis ran the plant and was showing signs of disengaging. Time to sit him down and set him straight before he went astray.

Find Sophia.

Repossess her car.

Nullify her ability to give evidence against him. Now that he thought about it, he realized he should have married her early on, when she was still enamoured with him. A wife couldn't be subpoenaed to give evidence against her husband.

He always made lists. Organization was the keystone to

his success. At the beginning of every week, he did an assessment of how the plant and distribution system was functioning and made a list of what needed his attention. His lists were getting longer and more complicated, the tasks he set himself more convoluted.

Perhaps it was time to shut things down and move the operation to another spot. The problem was, this was the perfect place. Where else would he find a hidden site for the plant next to a source of willing young workers?

There were some good reasons he was here. *Should he stay or should he go?* He snickered at the phrase from the silly song and folded the list, placing it in the front pocket of his jeans. He never left them around for anyone to find. Sophia thought he was an undercover cop. If he'd kept his temper, she wouldn't have taken off. He should have known he was out of control, but things had been going badly and it drove him crazy when that happened. Why should he have to take all the heat?

On the other hand, if she had any balls, she would have stayed with him. They lived a pretty good life. She hadn't worked since they arrived in Comox. He'd taken her to Mexico twice for a holiday. He gave her plenty of spending money. He flew her to Vancouver often to attend the theatre, have a luxury weekend in a good hotel or do some shopping. That car of hers was the best she'd ever driven, she said so often enough. She should have been tough enough to handle his moods. Apparently not.

So now he had to find her. Who to put on that job?

Aribadis was acting funny and couldn't necessarily be trusted. Perhaps it was time to up his pay. Anton certainly wasn't short of cash. His other man at the plant, Gerra, drove the van to pick up the workers. He wasn't bright enough to be given a task like this.

Leon was his partner. It wasn't really Leon's problem that Sophia had taken off. On the other hand, if this put their operation at risk, he had the right to know and give his own input on how to handle it.

Anton glanced at his watch. Where was Leon right now? Probably at Union Bay, working on the plane. It was where he liked to spend most of his day and the last time they talked he'd mentioned an oil change was on the schedule.

***

CHAPTER THIRTEEN

Rain's appointment at the police station in Nanaimo went off the rails from the very beginning. He was to meet with Detective Vickers, the cop in charge of the case, at two pm. When he got there, the detective wasn't available. He'd been called out of the detachment and no one knew where he was or when he might be back. He hadn't left a message for Rain, and the officer on the desk didn't seem willing to place a call to arrange anything else.

Rain left his new cell number for the detective and went back to his truck. As he climbed into the cab his personal phone rang. Brother Jake was on the line.

"Hi, bro," he answered. "What's the problem?"

He recognized Jake's laugh. "Do I only phone you when there's a problem?" his brother replied.

Rainier chuckled. "Yeah, pretty much."

"Okay, well not today. I'm going out to Vancouver on a course and thought I'd carry on over to the Island to see you when I'm finished."

"A course? What kind of course?"

"Private investigation. What else?" Jake had been pursuing a Private Investigator's licence for months, the main topic of conversation whenever they got together.

"Yeah, why am I not surprised?" Thoughtfully, Rain rubbed his jaw with rough fingers. "Listen, that could be of interest right now. It would be great to get together." He paused for a moment. "Jake, guess who's in town?"

"Couldn't say." Jake's voice sounded distracted.

"Thea Sophia Bonnar."

There was a short silence. "She is?" Jake sounded surprised. "You know, I'd heard she'd moved west. How did she find you?"

"Actually, I found her. She's staying at her Dad's house. Uncle Toby just took off on his long-awaited trip and she's staying there while he's gone."

"Okay, I heard he was going away. Southeast Asia, right? Listen, Rain. Dad's not too well. Did you know?"

Suddenly, Rain's breath left his lungs and he had trouble forcing words out in reply. "What do you mean? No one's said anything. I had a long conversation with him last week."

"Well, this just happened. They think he had a heart attack."

"What?" Rain gazed sightlessly through his windshield. Dad was lean and strong. He didn't gain weight, wasn't a heavy drinker, didn't smoke, and did a lot of physical labour. "How is that possible?"

"Yeah, my thought exactly. But they're saying he has high cholesterol and it hasn't been under control for a long time."

Rain blew out through pursed lips. "Did he know that?"

"Good question. You know what he's like. If the doc told him that, he probably just ignored it."

"Right." One stubborn dude, that was their father. "So what's the deal? Is he able to get around? Work? What?"

"Don't know." Jake sounded distant. "I'll find out more before I leave and fill you in when I get there, okay? Apparently he's home from the hospital, so it can't be that bad."

Just then Rain's police phone rang. "Okay, gotta go. See you soon, Jake. Find out what you can."

He disconnected and picked up the other phone from the cup holder on the dash. "Dexter Winston," he said, voicing his new name for the first time.

"Where the hell are you?" he heard in a heavy Scottish accent.

"Who is this?" Rain replied, holding back a sudden flash of temper.

"This is Detective Vickers. We were supposed to meet at two o'clock."

"Yeah, well you weren't there, so it's hard to meet if only one of us shows up." Rain hadn't even met this guy. He needed to smooth the waters if there was to be any hope of them working together. "I'm still sitting outside your detachment. I can be there in four minutes."

"Good, get a move on. Let's get this show on the road." There was more Scottish muttering and the line went dead.

Rain took the phone from his ear and stared at it a moment before clicking the off button and putting it in his pocket with the other one. Two phones, way more pressure than he needed.

Dad had a heart attack? He'd do some research and see what he could find out about that and the best approach for good results going forward.

***

CHAPTER FOURTEEN

Rain's meeting with Constable Vickers didn't go much better than their first phone call. By the time it was drawing to a close, he felt like he'd been interrogated for some imagined crime. The cop was belligerent and seemed clueless about what information should be passed on to him.

"Let's just sum this up," Rain said, leaning forward over the detective's desk in the common room, where three or four other officers were working at different tasks. The sound of ringing telephones was a constant background noise. "A young man came in to tell you he was being employed for cash and wanted to leave the work but was too intimidated. After interviewing him, you don't know where he works, what work he does, who pays him, or anything else of interest. Do you even know his name?" He jabbed his finger on the photo of the young man with the pimply chin. "A name would help me find him."

"I have a name," Vickers finally admitted with a smirk. "But I'm not goin' to give it to you. I don't want you goin' round to his house and alerting someone to our interest in him."

"In that case, what have you been able to do for him? From what I can see, he didn't get any benefit from telling you his tale. He's still working at this unknown place where he doesn't want to work, and being paid in cash."

The colour in Vickers fleshy cheeks was dark. He rocked back and forth in his chair. "I think he's still working there, yes. He could quit and just leave town, but he lives with his mother and he's afraid she might be in danger if he did that."

"Aha. So, you aren't protecting his mother, either. You've been a big help to him, I can tell."

"We can't just move him and his mother into protective custody for their personal safety," Vickers replied indignantly, his accent getting stronger with every word. 'We need evidence there's a real physical threat before we take those steps. Our budget isn't unlimited, you know."

"Okay, so have you set up surveillance on the Sunday van run? From what he says, that follows a schedule. Should be relatively easy to spot."

Vickers squirmed. "It's a tiny village. We can't park our cars and watch the road without drawing attention."

"I know what Cumberland looks like," Rain said. "I drove through there on my way here. You could certainly monitor the main road in and out of town. The evidence shows they travel quite a distance. If we find a van doesn't come in and out on Sunday or Thursday, then we monitor a different road."

"The road's narrow," Vickers argued. "You can't park a cop car there and go unnoticed."

"You don't use cop cars," Rain said sharply, his patience thinning. "It looked to me like there were various places where you could do surveillance from the protection of the forest at the side of the road. You could set up cameras that wouldn't even be noticed, and have a record of all the vehicles that go in and out of the village."

The Detective stopped twitching in his chair and focussed on his face. "Where?" he asked, pulling a map of the village of Cumberland from a pile of paper on his desk. "Show me."

"I'd need to go out there again with that in mind and take a closer look. Then I'll bring that information back to you. Give me a copy of the map and I'll use that. Deal?" Rain stood in frustration and held out his hand. All he had to do was get this show on the road. There was no end in sight to his probation if he couldn't come up with some useful information for the cops on this case.

After some hesitation, Vickers rose and shook his hand. "Deal," he said, handing over the tattered map.

***

CHAPTER FIFTEEN

Rain travelled the road leading into Cumberland, then out again, noting landmarks and spots with a potentially good view of the traffic. He settled on three different places where a camera could be positioned low enough to film the licence plates of passing vehicles while not being visible to the passing motorists. He marked them on the map, with notations as to why these spots worked. If Vickers cooperated, they had two or three days to get the equipment in place and begin recording information on the traffic before the van came through on Sunday, to pick up the workers and take them to their jobs.

He drove south to the Nanaimo detachment and left the map for Vickers at the office. The officer was out, so he wrote his cell number along the edge of the paper. He might need to order some business cards if this kept up. He stifled a chuckle. A card that would say what? *Call Dexter Winston to follow the money. Only on probation another few weeks, so act fast if you need his help.*

Heading south to Victoria, his spirits lifted. He'd see Sophia tonight, and Jake was booked to arrive tomorrow after he finished his course in Vancouver. It would be good to see his 'little' brother, though the news about Dad was worrisome.

Rain slowed for the Malahat Drive over the mountain, a part of the Island Highway famous for the number of accidents that occurred on it at any time of year, but especially in spring and fall with the dense fog that blanketed the area. He was pretty well used to the winding, curvy roads of British Columbia now. Where he was from in Saskatchewan, the roads were straight and square with directions north and south or east and west. You could literally see for miles in any direction. Here the hills and mountains, creeks and rivers caused the highways to curve and wind through valleys and forests. Yes, he'd heard the joke many times—if someone ahead of you was driving too slow, they must be from the Prairies. Not used to a bend in the road.

Soon he approached the outskirts of Victoria. He threaded the streets with care and parked his truck in the designated spot at the back of his building. It was a dated four-story structure in the Fairfield district that he'd purchased last year after the criminal charges against him were finally dealt with. The home had already been ruthlessly chopped into suites. He occupied the first floor of the place.

There was a reliable older woman named Bertha who rented one of the suites on the second floor, above him. She'd been there a long time and more or less ran the place. He didn't want to lose her as a tenant. Her presence meant he didn't have to pay attention to problems as they arose unless they were serious. Then he'd find Bertha on his doorstep or calling him hourly to tend to matters.

His suite was the largest in the house, but still smaller than anything he'd lived in in a long time. The bank loans officer hadn't been thrilled Rain had no steady job for reference on his mortgage application when he was in the process of purchasing it. But his half of the income from the commercial building he co-owned with Chloe Bowman more than made up for that, and the loan was quickly approved.

He glanced around, checking the other vehicles in the parking area. Bertha's car was in its spot, but the tenant in the basement had parked his truck in a way that blocked the space of his neighbour. He'd knock on his door and get him to move it. The house looked the same, although he could see some papers piled up in front of his door and the lawn needed mowing.

Grabbing his duffel bag, he lugged it up the short flight of stairs to his back door. He had a feeling of weightlessness. The case for Detective Cullen was starting to come together. It wouldn't be long now till he was free.

***

CHAPTER SIXTEEN

That night, Sophia was waiting on the front step when Rain pulled up in front of Toby's house. She climbed into the truck before he could get out and open the door for her. He put the gear in neutral with his foot on the brake and stared across as she fumbled for her seat belt. "In quite a hurry, there," he observed. "You could at least let me get parked."

She dimpled a grin at him. "You Prairie boys are always slow," she said, snapping the belt on.

"Slow on the uptake, or just slow?" he asked.

She gave him a sideways glance. "What's the difference?"

He smirked. "I'm not about to explain. You Prairie girls are often slow on the uptake." He shifted into gear to the sound of her exasperated snuffle. He'd almost forgotten how much fun it was to tease her.

When they got to the restaurant, she flounced out of the truck and marched toward the entrance without waiting for him. Jogging around the front of the vehicle, he caught her arm. He'd been looking forward to this evening, and it looked like it might go off track before he even got started. "Hold on, now. I was just teasing," he argued. "I didn't mean to hurt your feelings."

She glared up at him, plump lips pressed tightly together, little dimple flirting in the darkness. "I'd have to care to have my feelings hurt," she charged.

"True." Rain slid his fingers down the silky skin of her arm to grab her hand. "And the only reason you're going out to dinner with me is because you don't know anyone else in town."

She laughed and he felt her relax. "Not exactly. I've met some new people at my job."

"Huh." He glanced toward the door of the restaurant to give himself time to think. He didn't know anything about a job. "So the only reason you're going for dinner with me is pity. You feel sorry for me." He wrapped his arm around her shoulders. "I don't feel sorry for me if I get to eat dinner with you. I'm pretty pleased with myself."

She grinned and leaned into his side. "Rain Man," she said, "you're usually pretty pleased with yourself, as I recall."

"Ouch," he said. "That hurt. Are you still going to eat dinner with me?"

"I guess so. I'm hungry."

"Yeah, me too. And I'm glad you chose Greek, I love moussaka, and baklava."

"Me too. Especially the baklava." Her expression turned impish, and Rain couldn't resist. He lowered his head and pressed a kiss to those beautiful lips. She took a swift breath and when he raised his head she was staring at him with a wide-eyed, startled look. He had the same stunned feeling in his gut.

"I'll just try that again," he said. Turning her to face him, he kissed her long and slow, his lips lingering on hers. "Almost as good as baklava," he murmured. He was surprised to get the words out, his tongue seemed all tangled in his mouth.

"Well." Sophia tugged at his hand and pulled him forward. "I'm starving and you're just lollygagging out here."

He allowed her to lead him into the restaurant, his heart thudding in his chest. After the greeter seated them and the waiter took their drinks order, Rain studied her suddenly rosy cheeks. Her gaze darted around, nervously avoiding his. Okay, so maybe he wasn't the only one affected by that kiss.

***

CHAPTER SEVENTEEN

Rain cleared his throat and glanced at Sophia across the table from him. "Are you still driving the Audi?"

Her eyes widened. "Yes, why?"

"It's a pretty noticeable car."

"I know. But I can't sell it." She picked at a cuticle with her fingernail.

"Why not?" Rain already knew why she couldn't sell it. He reached across the table and covered her hand with his to stop the fidgeting.

"There's a lien on it, and he won't take it off."

"Who, Anton Ganaye?" Her alarmed expression was all the confirmation he needed. "Are you running from him?"

"How do you know?" she whispered. "It's secret."

"Nothing's secret if you know where to look," he said.

"That's what I'm afraid of. He's a cop, I can't escape him."

"Who says?" He bristled and took a sip of his scotch to keep from blurting something he shouldn't. "No one has the right to hunt you, not even a cop. You know that, right?"

"Cops have their own code," she murmured, her gaze pinned to a spot on the tablecloth between them.

"Do they?" He thought about that for a moment. Not what he'd seen from working with Detective Ross Cullen. Cops obeyed the law, even when it didn't aid their case.

"Why don't you drive your father's truck?" he asked. "That way you could leave your car in the garage until you decide what to do about it."

She gazed up at him eagerly, as if she were still ten years old and he'd just offered her an ice cream cone. He remembered that expression and it touched something deep inside him that he'd been trying hard to suppress for a long time.

"It would be great if I could drive it," she said. "I can't find the keys."

"I know where the keys are," he offered, squeezing her fingers and letting go to sit back.

The food had arrived. He took a deep breath, sniffing the aromas of the colourful array on his plate. Perfect. Good food, good scotch, some good wine on its way, and Sophia having dinner with him. He hadn't been able to stop thinking about how she'd looked that day showering on Toby's deck before climbing into the hot tub. Each time he laid eyes on her, it just reinforced the picture in his mind.

He moved restlessly in his chair and glanced up in time to

see her smile her thanks at the waiter, then watched the young guy's cheeks turn a dull red. He had to stifle a snort. *Get your own woman.*

"When I take you home, I'll show you where the keys are. Toby has a tiny safe in the back closet, where he keeps all kinds of things. Didn't he show you?"

Sophia shook her head. "There was a lot going on just before he left. I kind of arrived unexpectedly and it threw him off his plans."

"Hmm." Rain speared a piece of cucumber along with a chunk of feta cheese and popped it into his mouth. "I know a guy who'd buy your car, even with the lien on it," he offered.

She paused, her mouth open. "There's no way to sell that car with the lien. Anton made sure of that."

"Well, I know someone who knows someone," he said. "I used to buy and sell a lot of vehicles and I know a guy who can take it with the lien and move it on, if that's what you want. He won't pay you what you might get at a car dealer."

He wondered why he was offering this. It wasn't illegal. Someone would end up having to get the lien removed, but it did work. "How much is owed on it?" He already knew the answer to this question as well, and hoped the conversation didn't sound like an interrogation.

"Nothing." She shook her head. "It was just his way of controlling me. He gave me the car as a gift. Then the lien went on a few days later."

"But it's in your name, right?" He knew it was, having

received the search results from Motor Vehicles. Constable Dan Parker, Detective Cullen's right-hand man, had been very helpful in all his inquiries.

"Yes, the car's in my name. Mmm, this is so good."

He watched her lips close around the fork and had to look away. "Yeah," he agreed, "the food's good here. Can't wait for the baklava."

***

CHAPTER EIGHTEEN

The next day, Jake was booked on a late afternoon ferry from Vancouver and arrived at Rainier's place about five o'clock. He was sporting a new beard, groomed and shaved to the shape of a goatee, with a carefully clipped mustache. Must be the modern look of a PI.

Rain gave him a big hug and slap on the back, which was enthusiastically returned. The older he got, the more he valued his younger brother's company and opinions, not that he was willing to admit that out loud.

Jake had grown in the last few years, reaching his full height of an inch or two more than Rainier's six feet, and put on a few pounds of muscle in the interim. "Been working out?" Rain gave him a jab in the chest, which was instantly returned with enough force behind it to cause him to grunt in surprise.

"Maybe," Jake muttered, flexing his biceps. "Still trying to catch up to you."

"Huh," Rain said. "Wouldn't take much, bro. I've been

sidetracked with probation and all."

"Yeah? You look in pretty good shape."

Rain waved him into the apartment. "Want a beer?" He led the way into his small kitchen and opened the fridge. "I stocked up on your favourite." He pulled out two tall cans of a local brew and took a couple of mugs out of the freezer. "Come into the living room. More comfortable."

"You call this a living room?" Jake pulled a comical face at the sight of the small corner of his apartment containing a couch and one padded chair, along with a tiny coffee table. Rain elbowed him in the ribs. "Shut up and sit down, or I'll drink both of these myself."

Jake's laugh caused him to crack a smile. "You always were a pest," Rain muttered.

"And you were the easiest guy to bug," his brother replied.

"Yeah, I suppose. Susan was no fun, so we had to provide all the entertainment, right?"

"There's that." Jake relaxed into the only cushioned chair, so Rain sat on the couch and put the cans on the coffee table, pulling the tabs to a low hiss. "So, how was the course?" He poured beer into a mug and passed it over. "Worth coming here for?"

Jake took a long swallow and sighed loudly. "It was great. I learned a ton of stuff. The laws in BC are a little different from Saskatchewan, so that was good to know."

Rain raised a brow. "The laws in BC. Does that mean you'll be opening up business out here rather than back home?"

"Back home, eh?" Jake mimicked. "Do you still think of it that way? You haven't lived in Saskatchewan for more than six years."

"I know. Old habits," he replied. "I'm kind of hooked on the west coast now."

"You mean the wet coast, right?" They chuckled together and sipped beer in silence for a few moments. "The thing is, Rain Man, I'm thinking of opening a private investigator's office in the west and taking on a partner."

"Holy. So you are leaving home. What brought that on?" Rain gazed in amazement at his brother. "This is news. Do Mum and Dad know?"

"Not yet." Jake looked alarmed and they both shrugged. "I won't tell if you don't."

"Believe me, I won't tell," Rain replied. "I remember the response when I announced I was leaving."

"Yeah, me too. But my partner lives here, so it makes sense to open shop where he lives."

"Okay." Rain took another sip. "Do I know this fellow?"

"Probably better than I do," Jake replied.

Rain felt a small premonition whiz around in his brain. "What are you saying?"

"I'm saying, you should form a partnership with me. The Murdoch Investigators."

Rain gave a startled laugh. "Wasn't there a TV series with that title? The Murdoch Mysteries."

Jake shrugged. "Might have been. But it's our name, we can use it if we want. I'd like to be in business with you."

Rain gave his brother a penetrating stare even as he felt excitement stir in his chest. A chance to continue to untangle problems, something he loved to do, while at the same time living in the open, instead of undercover as he had for years. "I'm not good news to be around, Jake. I have a criminal record, which won't go away, and the police will always be watching whatever I get involved with. It could put paid to your business before it even gets legs."

"Huh. Is that your best shot at putting me off? I happen to know you'll be through with probation about the same time I get my licence. I thought you liked solving puzzles, sorting out mysteries."

"I do, I do." He glanced into his beer mug which, to his surprise, was almost empty, and put it down on the coffee table. "I just don't want to jinx what you've been working so hard to achieve. You don't deserve that. Nor do I have the training that you're getting. I couldn't get licenced as a PI. How long before you get your licence? You must be close."

"Soon. And we only need one licence to open the company. There'd be time for you to work on your courses and get approved later, but it wouldn't stop you from working on any cases we had going."

Rain snorted. "I don't see why you'd hook up with a loser like me."

"You're no loser." Jake sat straight and slammed his empty mug down with a thump. "You're one of the smartest people I know. I want to open a business with you. You've got experience, you know how to make it work, you're organized. I need you."

"Whoa." Rain gazed down at his hands as he threaded his fingers together, then rubbed them down his face. He glanced at his brother. "I'm flattered, Jake. Let me think about it. I have to say that what I'm doing now for the police to finish off my probation is right down your alley. I can't tell you what it's about, but I'm learning a lot."

His brother nodded. "See what I mean? We could start out with a leg up because I'll have the licence and you'll have the experience. Win-win, I say."

Rain laughed. His brother's enthusiasm had always dragged him along, sometimes into situations that he hadn't properly thought through. He'd better put his thinking cap on this time and do a little research. He wasn't about to unwittingly jeopardize what Jake had put so much sweat equity into trying to create.

***

CHAPTER NINETEEN

Later, in a noisy downtown restaurant, they had been seated at a small corner table. Jake enthusiastically cut into his steak and took a healthy bite. Rain grinned. "People here tend to eat chicken and fish," he commented, then laughed out loud at the astounded expression on his brother's face.

"That's a shame," said Jake. "Why would they do that?"

"They live on the ocean. Lots of great seafood to be found. Salmon, halibut, mussels, oysters, even dogfish."

"Dogfish?" Jake gaped, then grinned ruefully. "You're pulling my leg."

"No, there's a fish called dogfish. A lot of people eat it, but it's primarily used to create fake crab meat."

"Huh." Jake cut another big slice of his steak. "I'm just a Prairie boy at heart."

"Yeah. My business partner, Chloe Bowman, threw a barbecue when Mum and Dad were in town last. They didn't touch the fish but did manage to mangle a good pile of beef. Speaking of which, how are the folks?"

Jake laid his utensils down and clasped his hands together as he leaned across the table. "Mum's fine. Dad is on the mend. He sleeps a lot, sleeps long at night and needs a nap in the middle of the day. The doc says that should ease up after a time. It's how the body deals with the type of damage he's suffered. His heart is strong. Doc is happy with his physical condition and the way he's responded to his new medications. But he doesn't want him farming any longer. Too demanding on his energy."

"Whoa. That's news. He won't take that well. Not farm? But the crop is already planted, right? He told me so the other day when we were talking. Wouldn't discuss the heart attack though. I couldn't pry anything out of him on that issue."

"No, this information is all from Mum. She started going with him on his doctor visits because Dad wouldn't tell her anything either. Probably knew she'd step in and drag him off the farm."

Rain considered for a moment. "It'll be a shame to let the old homestead go and never lay eyes on that place again. I guess we'd better plan on being out there for harvest this fall. No way we can leave it in his hands."

"Yep, good idea." Jake waved at the waiter and ordered dessert.

"How do you stay so slim? Must be built like Dad," Rain grumbled.

His brother laughed. "I'm built just like you. Long and lean, kind of like Dad, I guess. But I've been so busy in the last few months, I haven't had time to turn around, let alone worry about my weight."

"I have an idea about your office," Rain offered.

Jake paused and focussed narrowly on his face. "Our office," he corrected.

"Okay, our office."

At that Jake gave a whoop and reached his hand across the table. "Shake on it, Rain. Shake on it and we're committed."

Rain chuckled and shook his head. "I haven't had time to think it through yet. Give me a day or so."

"Hmm" he said, retracting his hand. "A day sounds iffy. You could change your mind in that amount of time."

"Well, about the office. This building that I own with my business partner—"

"Yeah, where is it anyway? I'd like to see what it looks like."

"We could go there tomorrow, do a walk through...."

"Can't," Jake interjected. "I'm reserved on the first ferry out tomorrow morning, got to get back to work before I lose my job."

"Okay." Rain waited until the chocolate torte was placed in front of him. "Still with the delivery service?"

"Right. Coming up on five years. I'll stay there until I'm ready to open the business. It's flexible hours, pays well, worth hanging onto. So, what about the office?"

"Right." Rain took a bite of his dessert. "This commercial building has an empty space at the back that we haven't leased yet. Not very big, but there are a couple of offices, a staff room, washrooms. It could work for a private investigators' business. You'd need someone in the office for reception, and there's room for that in the entrance. If we drive by on our way home, we can't go in, but you could get an idea of what it's like."

"Wow." Jake was almost bouncing with excitement. "Sounds great, but we aren't ready yet, and probably can't afford the cost at the start-up of our company."

"I know the owners," said Rain with a hint of mischief in his voice. "You can probably rent it for the cost of utilities to get things going." He revelled in the pleased expression on his brother's face. Now all he had to do was decide if he wanted to be a part of this endeavour. He hadn't exactly paid much attention to what his own plans were after probation, always maintaining his focus on just getting through it successfully. The angst and irritation of his situation had him off balance most of the time—reporting to a probation officer, being at the beck and call of Detective Ross Cullen, jumping when told to. It hadn't been easy to deal with.

But the end was near and it was time to take a close look at where he was headed. If Sophia was going to stay in town, he mused, all the more reason to set up shop here. The idea was startling. When had he decided that? And he didn't even know if she was staying, but the picture of the naked woman having her shower that was fixed in his mind....

***

CHAPTER TWENTY

The brothers rose together early in the morning. Soon Jake headed out in his battered and rusty brown truck with the red box to catch the ferry to the mainland. At the same time, Rainier left town, driving his undercover car through remarkably light traffic up the Malahat, where miraculously it was dry. The daily storm hadn't passed through yet. This highway was always under construction— a new engineering plan was created every couple of years, ostensibly designed to calm traffic, but usually only succeeding in enraging the drivers.

On the journey, Rain pondered his conversation with Jake. His brother had reminded him of the funeral for Thea Sophia's younger brother, Pete. Pete had died the year before and Rain hadn't been able to return to Saskatchewan for the service. The police had been after him at that point. He hadn't been free to go home, or even contact family for fear of being caught. What he hadn't known was how the young Bonnar had died. He'd gotten hooked on meth and ended up in a fight with a drug gang. They'd killed him. Nor had anyone been charged with the crime.

The whole scenario gnawed at Rain. Why didn't he know this about Pete Bonnar? Too much going on in his life, he figured, with the death of his business partner, and the effort to stay undercover and out of reach of the cops. But it would explain Sophia's tears when they talked about her younger brothers and sister the other night.

Meth was a devastating drug, its addiction factor was fast and high. Some people said they were hooked after one try. And the people who sold it were brutal in their approach. There was no room for a misstep on the part of the drug user. He should know. He'd stayed with his girlfriend Trudy long after she'd begun her addiction struggles, wondering how it would end, if it would end. It had been devastating for both of them.

Rain arrived at the Nanaimo police station before eight o'clock for his meeting with Detective Vickers. The cop wasn't there. Rain gritted his teeth. The lack of cooperation from this officer was starting to grate.

When he explained at the front counter the purpose of his visit, an attractive female officer found him a desk in the common room and set up the camera recordings from the Cumberland road surveillance for him to watch. At least Vickers had followed through with the plan for camera surveillance. Rain was finally in gear on this investigation. The officer brought him a coffee before she left with her partner for a shift on highway patrol.

One of the cops at the next desk called over. "Bet you're not so ticked off at Vickers now. Most of us would give our eye teeth to have Constable Marlyse look after us."

Rain grinned and shrugged his shoulders. "She seemed very nice. But Vickers was supposed to meet me here this morning to get the show on the road."

The cop shook his head. "Vickers is off duty today. No way was he coming in on his day off to look after a civilian."

Rage rose from Rain's gut in a rolling wave. "Vickers is quite a piece of work," he snapped. "He's supposed to be communicating with me, and makes appointments but never shows up. How does he keep his job?"

The cop gave him a level look. "Best to keep your shirt on, fella."

"Right." Rainier focussed on the screen in front of him as the heat in his chest slowly receded. He'd keep his shirt on if it killed him. All he had to do was finish this case.

An hour later, he shifted and flexed the muscles in his back in the overly warm, slightly clammy atmosphere. This was tough work—sit still and watch. Luckily, the road into Cumberland wasn't that busy. He'd started skipping the recording ahead till he saw the next vehicle show up, then slowing it down to examine each one. In older vehicles, the driver was often clearly visible. But the newer ones all had darkened glass, making it impossible to see the driver. He memorised the cars going through, looking for those that appeared more often.

He got to Thursday's recordings and fast forwarded to the last half of the day. If the workers were being brought home, it was likely after at least some hours of work in the bunker. He didn't know it was a bunker, but that was all he could imagine, given the information the young man had told Vickers. Some kind of underground structure, likely with pipes through the roof for ventilation. Not only that, but the information said they always travelled in the dark, so the last half of the day was of more interest.

Rain caught a few late-model vehicles coming and going, mostly pickup trucks, some with crew cabs and fancy gear attached to headache bars in the back. He isolated a view of the licence plates and printed off the shots, recording the numbers in his notebook.

The sky had already darkened on-screen by the time something else of interest appeared. A new-looking van passed by the first camera. The windows were darkened but there must have been a light on inside, because Rain could see there were at least four passengers plus the driver. Most of the riders looked like young males, judging from the wild hair and full beards. He sent the shot to be printed.

The next two cameras picked up the van within minutes, but the inside light had been turned out and there was no new information to be had as to who was riding in it. He caught a shot of the licence plate on the last camera and recorded it with the others.

Continuing to watch, he observed the same van leaving Cumberland a little over thirty minutes later. He glanced around the almost silent room. Two of the cops had departed for their shifts and a third had arrived.

Rain rose and approached the new occupant at his desk. "I need to run some licence plate numbers. How do I do that?"

The officer gave him a considering look, then accompanied him back to his desk. "You're the guy working with Vickers on the meth issue, right?" At Rain's nod, he booted up the computer and logged into a separate site. "Here you go. Motor vehicle information—licences, ownership, registration, names and addresses. Good luck with Vickers. Not the most cooperative guy we've got stationed here."

"That's for sure," Rain muttered.

The cop paused and gave a bark of laughter. "I'm Morse," he said. "If you need something and can't get it, talk to me." He pulled out a business card and laid it on the desk. "My feelings aren't tender, so if you don't call, that's fine too. But it would be nice to get somewhere on that case. We've had various people looking at it for a long time."

"Okay." Rain studied the card. *Detective John Morse, Nanaimo RCMP.* "I'll call if I need something. Thanks for that. I appreciate it."

***

CHAPTER TWENTY-ONE

Rain pulled up his chair in the nearly empty common room and started work on the licence plate numbers he'd pulled off the screen. The phone noise around him had diminished greatly and the parade of officers marching through had rolled back to a thin trickle. By the end of the morning, he had a short list of 'people of interest.' The three trucks he'd zeroed in on were all owned by young men, between the ages of nineteen and twenty-one. The van was owned by a fellow in his thirties.

Rain's next task was to run them through the police charges file and see who carried a record. He hunched his shoulders at the thought. His own record would show up any time someone did a search on him. As it turned out, none of these young men had a police record, just a few speeding tickets. However the van owner, Gerra Papillion, was Mexican, so he might have had a record elsewhere but Rain had no access to that information.

Then he looked at addresses. The truck owners all lived in Cumberland. That might signal some or all of them worked for this undercover operation. Papillion had given an address in Union Bay. Rain had never been to Union Bay and didn't know what it was like although he found it on the map. He added it to his list of tasks to cover in the next few days. He moved restlessly. When was he going to have some time to spend with Sophia? Didn't ordinary people have a life?

Finally, he opened up the camera recordings again, jumping ahead to Sunday. Their informant had said the workers were taken out of Cumberland Sunday night and returned Thursday night. Sure enough. Sunday evening showed a similar van going along the road toward Cumberland, but it was raining heavily and the image wasn't clear. Same for the return journey a half hour later. The dim light and heavy rain meant he couldn't see if there were the same number of young men in the van. Not only that, the windows were shaded so he couldn't see inside the vehicle. But he took it as a good sign that the van had done the run they'd been informed about. The picture of the licence plate was foggy but it appeared to be the same vehicle.

He wondered how that young man, their informant, was doing—having taken the risk of giving his information to the cops but still caught on the treadmill of work that he hated and wanted to quit. The fear must eat at him daily.

At least Rain had something to present to Ross Cullen when he returned to Victoria. The next step would be up to the cops, surely. Rain's role was to follow the money. Besides, he wanted to research Anton Ganaye, the guy who might be tracking Sophia. No one, not even a cop, had the right to do that to a young woman, to threaten and harass. The fact she was living alone in her father's house bothered him mightily, especially now that he was out of town half the time.

His first impulse was to invite her to move in with him, to ensure her safety. Then he could keep an eye on her. But of course, that wasn't all he wanted to do, so he'd kept quiet. His place wasn't really designed to share. If he took over one of the other units in the chopped-up-house and added it to his, it would give him more space. On the other hand, all his tenants had been there a lot longer than he had.

Bertha shouldered most of the responsibility for the place. She swept the common hallways and staircases every day and picked up any litter in the yard. The other second floor unit was occupied by a young fellow in the navy, who was away at sea half the year, knowing his apartment was secure. The older fellow in the basement had quite a bit of room but was limited by smaller windows high up in the walls. He took care of the yard, mowed the lawn and weeded the flower beds. He also did his own vegetable patch in the back, which Rain especially liked. He'd been encouraged to help himself to the fare—a healthy combination of beans, squash, tomatoes and kale.

The units at the very top of the house were always occupied by university students, who usually shared accommodation. No one else seemed interested in climbing all those stairs. They came and went at all hours, with their varied courses and odd part-time jobs. Bertha took care of that too, ensuring the noise-level never reached stratospheric proportions.

All in all, it worked rather well. But not if he wanted a woman to move in with him. His place was too small to be comfortable. Maybe he'd have to find another house if

Thea Sophia were to agree to live with him. It wasn't as if he couldn't afford it. Houses were expensive on Vancouver Island, but his half of the income from the commercial building had been piling up unnoticed in his account. The police paid him for his probationary services, which more or less covered his current costs. They'd supplied an undercover cop car, cell phone and credit card for meals, gas and hotels as needed. What more was there?

He glanced down at his frayed jeans and well-worn boots. Perhaps an upgrade in clothes might be in order. He couldn't court a woman while looking like he could hardly afford to buy her dinner. The idea gave him a sharp jolt in his chest. When had he made the decision to court Sophia? He'd been toying with the idea for some time, but must have recently reached a decision. He just hadn't been aware of it.

He glanced uneasily around the common room. Most of the cops had departed. Morse was just gathering a bundle of papers and shutting down his computer.

Rain rose to take a break, pulling his sweaty shirt away from his chest in the close air.

"Finished?" Morse called.

"Not quite," said Rain. "Still got a bit to go. Just need the facilities."

Morse nodded toward the corridor at the rear. "Right down there. See you later."

Back in his chair a few minutes later, Rain found the common room empty. Good. Time to search out what information he could about Anton. An hour passed before he gusted a sigh and sat back. Ganaye lived in Comox, according to his drivers' licence information. And he drove a new black pickup truck. No criminal record, just a few driving infractions. No employment to speak of. He'd have to ask Sophia, but it would be Detective Ross Cullen who would be able to confirm or deny the undercover cop story that he hid behind. Rain noted the licence number for Ganaye's vehicle and stood. Time to find out more about this guy. Then he'd head down island to report to Cullen.

Driving further north, Rainier found Ganaye's Comox address. He located the small bungalow on a quiet dead-end street, gave it a visual once over and snapped a few photos. No black pickup in sight. There was a single-car garage attached to the house and the pickup could be parked in there. But when he walked down the side of the structure and peered in the dusty window, the space was empty. If Ganaye was at work, Rain had no idea where that might be.

***

CHAPTER TWENTY-TWO

Anton sat at his kitchen table, a pad of paper in front of him. His pen was at the ready but he hadn't picked it up yet. What would his list say today? The last week had been frantic, he felt like he must have taken care of pretty well anything that could go wrong with his enterprise.

First, the power went off at the plant. With no lights, it was pitch black in there. There weren't any windows and the door was blocked to maintain their privacy. Of course, no work could be done if the workers couldn't see. It was too dangerous. Aribadis had called to let him know they'd started up the generator but didn't have enough fuel to last more than a day. The noise was an issue, and the generator produced fumes that they were struggling to blow out of the place without attracting attention.

He should have known this would be the result of his machinations. When they first set up shop, Gerra had offered to access the power for them. He'd run a line to the nearest power pole and hacked into the supply. Free electricity. It was great. They didn't have to pay for it, nor did they have to let the power service know where they were located.

However, the power draw must have been noticed, because upon inspection, Anton discovered their illegal line had been removed. Gerra had run the line into the plant in a trench that he dug, but the power line guys hadn't bothered digging it up. They'd just disconnected it at the pole and cut the line where it disappeared into the ground. That was actually good news, because if they'd bothered to follow the line along the ditch, they would have discovered the plant. Disaster, right there.

Union Bay had been a viable establishment at one time, but not anymore. There were empty and derelict structures on nearly every street and road. About a kilometre and a half from the entrance to the plant was an ancient warehouse building that had been empty as long as he'd been here. Anton found the old guy who owned it and made a deal to rent it for a surprisingly low rate by offering to pay a year's worth of rent up front. The owner, when they met up to walk through the premises and hand over the keys, was ecstatic. "Never thought I'd be able to rent this thing again. It's been empty for years. Will likely need some upgrades. What do you plan to use if for?"

Just the question Anton didn't want to answer. "Gerra has some plans," he replied, pointing to his van driver. "Don't know if it will be used for storage or factory work."

The old guy raised bushy grey brows, handed over the key, and quickly pocketed the envelope of cash Anton gave him.

The first thing they did was call the power company to get the feed hooked up. He'd decided to call Leon in to handle that part. No reason why he had to do it all. By the end of the week, power had been provided in Leon's name, and Gerra had run a long feed for the electricity back into the plant. Things were up and running again.

Anton looked at the blank page in front of him and picked up the pen. He began to write.

Get water supplied to the building. It would be like a red flag if they rented the building but didn't actually use it. All their neighbours would be looking to see what they did with the building. Union Bay was a small community and information like that would race like wild fire about the place.

Move some furniture into the building. He wanted it to look legitimate, even if Gerra was the only one occupying it.

Get another dog to guard the premises. Gerra handled all the dogs, he could always move in and keep the new animal with him. Anton didn't want anyone snooping around the old building to discover it was still empty.

Find Sophia. He scratched that out. If she was really gone and never coming back, then so be it. Even if he found her, he couldn't force her to remain with him. The car was gone too. That thought bothered him mightily.

Find Sophia's car. That made more sense.

Folding the list, he forcefully shoved it into the front pocket of his jeans.

***

CHAPTER TWENTY-THREE

Sophia checked herself in the bathroom mirror. Her outfit looked great—a short mauve skirt with a swirl to the hem and a sleeveless V-necked silk blouse in a deeper violet tone. Maybe Rain would be in town in time to go for dinner. She took one more swipe at her hair with the brush and coated her lips with a pale pink lipstick. Nothing too outlandish when working for the police. She smiled to herself.

Rain had been so helpful, locating the keys to Dad's truck. She had finally begun to relax. Her car was hidden in the garage where there were no windows to peer in, she had a job so she could begin to make some money, and she'd obtained a cell phone with a new number. She'd sent out texts to everyone to let them know her contact info. Further, Rain was in her corner. Something leaped under her breast, a feeling of rising excitement. It had always been hard to get Rain's attention, but now it seemed it was hers for the asking.

How long would that last? He had been a busy guy back home, all the hockey practices, and meetings with the debating team, time with his buddies. She didn't know what the future would bring, but decided to enjoy the attention while she could. She grabbed a light jacket from the front closet and shrugged it on. Picking up her purse, she took the truck keys out of the side pocket.

As she headed for the front door, she glanced out the window and paused mid-stride. There was a black pickup truck parked across the street, with someone large and bulky sitting in the front seat. The windshield was too dark to see the driver's face, but she recognized that truck and the licence plate. Anton had found her. Fear rose like a tide, swamping her in its path. She sat on the stairs and peeked around the side of the window-frame to check. Yes, it was definitely Anton's truck.

She wasn't totally surprised— in fact, had been anticipating this for a while. He knew her father lived in Victoria. He would know she'd probably end up on Dad's doorstep. Hopefully he wasn't aware that Toby Bonnar was out of town. Maybe she should have gone back to Moose Jaw, and joined her younger siblings there.

Silently, she crept forward to make sure the front door was locked, then tiptoed into the hallway. Turning, she walked to the rear of the house and out the back door. She glanced around. From where Anton was parked, he'd be unable to see into the backyard, and the good news was there was a curve in the street toward the right. She glanced that way and shuddered. There were some high fences between the rear yards in that direction. She looked down at her tan pumps. The heels weren't too high, and she was a Prairie girl. She could do this. All she had to do was cross over a couple of yards and get to the intersection.

Two minutes later, she stood on the sidewalk of the next street over, to the sound of dogs barking madly behind her. She'd discovered a low fence at the end of Dad's yard and walked through his neighbour's place to the street opposite. No need to climb those high fences. On the other hand, she hadn't been aware they had dogs. With any luck, Anton wouldn't be alerted to her presence by the noise. With a clammy hand, she fumbled in her purse for her phone and pressed Rain's contact information. He answered on the second ring.

"Sophia?"

His deep voice caused an excited jolt in her breast. "Hi, Rain. I wondered if you could come give me a ride to work this morning."

"To work?" he questioned. "I'm in Nanaimo."

"Oh. Sorry."

"No, that's all right. Isn't Toby's truck working?"

"Not at the moment. I'll fill you in when I see you."

He seemed to think about that. "Can you take a cab? I could come by to look at the truck when I get home, see what the problem is, but I'm not sure when that will be."

"Good idea," she said. "Maybe I'll see you tonight."

"I'd like that," he rasped in his rough voice. Immediately, an answering shiver took up room in her belly. "I'll call you to let you know what the plans are," he continued. "Are you okay?"

"Great," she said. "I'm fine. I'll wait for your call."

Just as she pressed off, a bus turned the corner and stopped on the other side of the street. Sophia made a run for it, boarding just before the doors closed.

***

CHAPTER TWENTY-FOUR

Anton started his truck and drove north to find Leon at the float plane dock in Union Bay. The trip to Victoria had been a waste of time. Although he'd found Sophia's father's place, he hadn't found Sophia. At one point, he was sure he saw movement inside the house, but no one came out and the truck stayed where it was parked in the drive. Finally losing patience, he got out of his vehicle and rang the doorbell but there was no response. It was a small rural street and he felt exposed sitting on the tarmac watching the door. Perhaps there was a better way to find her.

Union Bay was a small community, seldom much activity at the docks except when fishing season opened. Then engines revved and boats lined up at the fuel station before heading out to sea. Right now, one fellow rested on an overturned bucket at the gas dock, his eyes closed as he leaned against the gas pump and waited for his next customer.

The orange engine hatch of their plane was propped open and Leon's head was stuck in the housing, his thick body leaning against the exterior frame. Leon had come into their joint business at the beginning, using his money to match Anton's to pay for supplies and get things underway. But he'd lost interest fast. Now his main focus seemed to be on the plane— his new favourite friend. Anton snorted in disgust.

"Leon," he said, tapping his shoulder. "How are things?"

Leon startled and yanked his head out of the cowling, cracking his skull on the upright. "Anton. Don't creep up on me like that."

He frowned. "I didn't creep. I made enough noise coming down the ramp to wake the dead. Maybe you need to start paying attention to something besides this plane, nice as it is."

"Why would I? You've got everything under control."

"True." He nodded at the wing of the plane. "Are we ready for the trip to Vancouver tomorrow? The supply is piling up and I don't like to keep so much on hand at any one time. Too dangerous. Our buyer is getting antsy."

"Yup. Ready to go. I've already filed the flight plan."

A shiver crawled up Anton's spine. Flight plans were never a good idea. Yes, they were required, but better to be devious. For instance, take off flying south and file the plan saying they were travelling from Duncan or Cowichan Bay. That way they didn't leave a trail of flights out of Union Bay to Vancouver and Seattle. Leon never seemed to understand that.

"I usually file the flight plan," he reminded his partner.

"Yeah, well, this one's already done."

"Okay. I need to talk to you. Some things have changed."

Leon got a wary look on his face. "What things?"

"Just some things."

"Okay. Like what?"

"Sophia's gone."

Leon shrugged. "I figured. Where'd she go?"

"Don't know. Haven't found her yet. How did you know?"

"You've been more jumpy than usual, and I haven't seen her in a bit. Just figured."

"Hmm." Anton fingered his goatee as he studied his partner. Did Leon have something to do with her leaving so suddenly? He was beginning to realize he didn't trust his partner the way he used to. "Have you heard from her?"

Leon snorted. "I never talked to her when she was here. Why would I hear from her after she left?"

"*Have you heard from her?*" he bellowed, grabbing Leon's arm. Then he backed off and glanced swiftly around, wondering who might have witnessed his sudden surge of temper. It had been a while since he'd lost control like that, and it had been Sophia who'd taken the brunt each time.

Leon levelled a look at him and shook his head. "You're getting out of hand, Anton," he muttered. "I don't need this. You never should have taken her on in the first place. There we were, just starting up and you get yourself a piece of arm candy. She wasn't necessary."

"You might not have thought so," he muttered. "If you want

to live like a monk, that's your problem."

Leon glowered. "So, you've lost your woman. That's not good news. Wonder what she knows?" His expression was sardonic. "What else did you want to tell me?" he growled.

Anton muttered a few choice words under his breath and dug the toe of his worn boot into the faded wood of the dock. "I think there might be someone siphoning product off. The numbers have fallen. Don't know if it's Aribadis, or who. Any ideas? Have you noticed anything out of the norm?" he asked hopefully. Not that Leon paid any attention. He gave the accounts a cursory glance every month and took his share of the cash, no questions asked.

Leon raised his bushy brows. "No, I know we aren't making as much money. But I also know that supplies are harder to come by and they cost more."

"Yeah." They shared a gloomy look. Just then Anton jumped as a siren erupted from his pocket. A similar ringing began from Leon's chest.

"What the fuck?" Leon tugged his phone from his breast pocket and stared at it angrily.

Anton grabbed his cell from his jeans, shut off the sound and turned to run. "It's the alarm. Something's happened at the plant."

The ringing behind him stopped and he heard Leon call, "I'll leave you to it. Let me know."

He kept going, climbed into his truck and started it up. Slamming it into gear, he spun gravel beneath the tires before they gripped the road and the truck shot forward. After this, he vowed, he would cut Leon out of the operation permanently. No way was he going to carry the whole load for a partner who had lost interest. On the other hand, there might not be any load to carry, depending on what he found at the plant.

***

CHAPTER TWENTY-FIVE

Rain's plan was simple—follow the van. Vickers didn't seem to think it could be done, but Rainier figured he'd do it himself if he couldn't get any cooperation from the police. There wasn't an easier way to find where the workers were going, unless they could put a tracker on the vehicle. That was also one of the options he was considering. If the cops added a few more cameras, they'd soon know which houses the van stopped at to pick up a worker. They could choose the best spot, hide an operative nearby and attach a tracker on the bumper when the van was halted on the street waiting for the young men to board. Yes, someone might notice the undercover activity, but by the time the tracker was found and discarded, they would have followed the van and have the information they needed about where it went.

Why hadn't Vickers done this before now? Rain didn't know and didn't care enough to ask. It wasn't likely he'd get an answer, anyway. He had the go ahead from Cullen to move forward on his ideas. If Vickers couldn't come up with an undercover cop car and have one of his men trail the van, Rain would do it himself. Anything to get this case solved. It meant being in position on the edge of Cumberland early Sunday night when the vehicle left town with its cargo of young workers. Rain identified an old logging road that showed little signs of use. This was where he would choose to wait if he had to.

He drove down-island for home, knowing he might well be on his way back to Cumberland in a few days. Time to get this show on the road. He wanted the case closed before Jake returned to town with his PI licence in hand. He wanted to spend time with Sophia, to explore a possible relationship with her. He wanted a life.

Before he passed through Duncan his cop cell phone rang, and he punched the button on the dash to answer. It was Morse from the Nanaimo detachment. "Murdoch," he said, "there's been a development I thought you should know about. Where are you now?"

"I'm on the highway just north of Duncan, heading south," Rain said.

"Good." Morse replied. "Glad I caught you before you ended up back in Victoria. There was a fire, and a couple of young men have landed in the hospital. Badly burned. We don't know where the fire occurred. These kids were just dropped off in the parking lot of the hospital here in Nanaimo, so we don't have a lot of information. They're both in rough shape. Neither one of them is in condition to give us the information we need to investigate what has happened."

"I see." Rain pulled to the side of the road, and put his car in neutral, his foot on the brake, keeping an eye on the rear-view mirror. In his opinion, it paid to be careful, and he always watched to see if anyone was following him. "How does this connect with the case? I'm assuming that's what you're calling me about."

"Right. Well this looks textbook for a meth lab fire. No one hung around to look after them, just brought them to emergency and dumped them off in the parking lot, then left in a hurry. It was obviously a flash fire, their skin and clothing totally consumed by it."

"Holy shit." Rain rubbed a hand over the stubble on his chin. "I see what you mean. I should turn around and see if I can question these guys. How old are they?"

"Yeah, you should. They both had IDs on them, that was all they had—no money, credit cards, business cards, just driver's licences. One's nineteen, one is twenty. We'll be talking to their families, of course, but if you could see what you can discover from talking to them—might have more luck than a police officer, know what I mean?"

"Yeah. Got it. I'll be there in a few."

"No rush," Morse replied. "They aren't going anywhere."

Rain disconnected and stared unseeing through his windshield at the dying sun. He'd better get hold of Sophia on her new cell phone. They were to go for dinner tonight. Now it was likely he wouldn't even get home till tomorrow. He hoped Toby's truck wasn't giving her any more problems.

***

CHAPTER TWENTY-SIX

At Union Bay, Anton shoved his key into the ignition and waited for Leon to put his into the slot beside it. He'd purposely had the plane engineered this way—it took two keys to start it up. One of the owners couldn't take off with the plane without the other's cooperation or consent. Some would say it was a lack of trust, but Anton saw it as good planning. He donned the head gear and strapped himself into his seat. The dock hand released their ties, casting them adrift.

He took control of the plane, using the propeller wash to push them away from the wharf toward the open water ahead. The cargo was stashed in the back. Luckily he kept it at his house, or there would be nothing to take with them to sell to their buyer on this trip. The fire in the cave had been horrific. Certainly the latest batch of meth was toast.

He checked around them and shoved the levers forward as the engines roared for takeoff. Soon they were flying above the swirl of boats and tiny islands below, heading for the big city.

"How did the alarm at the plant work out?" Leon called to him. "Was it a fire?"

"Yeah, it was a fire. Two workers in hospital, this week's batch lost."

Leon whistled through his teeth as he pulled up the chart on the dash to plot their trajectory. "That's not good. How did they get to hospital?"

"Aribadis took them."

"Huh." Leon adjusted their direction. "You can't just walk into a hospital and check people in."

"He's not stupid. He dropped them in the entry and drove away. The problem, asshole, is that as they recover, they'll be interrogated by the cops. They aren't stupid either. They'll recognize those burns for what they are."

Leon shot him a glare but didn't reply.

"We might have reached a stage where it's time to close shop," Anton continued inTO his mic, over the noise of the engines. "We can open up elsewhere. We don't need to hire as many employees. We can probably do the work ourselves with a couple of helpers. We'd produce less but payroll would be less, and the profit possibly higher."

More silence. Anton wasn't surprised. Leon wouldn't welcome actually working in the business. He focussed on the ferry below, plowing its way through the strait, with a small pod of dolphins surfing in its wake. The west coast was a beautiful place to live, no question. Maybe he could get rid of the whole operation, ditch Leon and go from there. He had all the sources and contacts he needed to establish the business again wherever he chose. As a single operator he could support himself in the style to which he'd become accustomed. He smirked at the idea.

Glancing over, he wondered if Leon was thinking similar thoughts. Probably not. He doubted his partner could set up shop, he'd paid so little attention to the operation of the plant right from the start.

On the other side of the water, they tied up at the public wharf at Steveston near downtown Vancouver. Their contact was scheduled to meet them in the parking lot of the market, so they each hefted a large backpack and headed up the ramp. While they waited for someone to make contact, Leon prowled impatiently up and down while Anton leaned against a post and surveyed the area. Soon the delivery truck he'd been watching for eased into the lot and found a parking spot nearby. Anton straightened, waved to the driver and strolled toward him, Leon trailing behind. "About time," he heard his partner mutter. Yes, it was about time to end this charade and look for a new beginning. His patience was gone. It appeared Leon's was too.

The driver's door slid open, and Anton could see inside. "Brad," he said. "Good to see you. Hope all is well."

"Not bad," Brad replied. He was a slim, middle-aged man with thinning grey hair, who had been doing deliveries for twenty years before he'd found a way to augment his income. He climbed out and walked around to the back to open the doors. "More privacy back here," he muttered. "What have you got for me?"

"Quite a bit." He motioned Leon forward. "Two packs, so more than usual. But we've had a problem at the plant, so it's going to be less next time."

Brad opened the first pack and peeked inside at the plastic wrapped parcels they presented. "Well, this looks good.

Let's see the other one." He pawed through, then tossed the packs forward into the hold of the truck, drawing several bags toward them. He gestured with his hand. "This is all I have for you. It's a little harder to get supplies these days. Best I could do, I'm afraid."

Anton looked at the small pile of packages, making out bottles of ammonia and iodine, some cans of paint thinner and drain cleaner in the mix. "That's it?" He gave Brad an incredulous look. "You're our supplier. Where are the cold meds? This doesn't look like you've done your job. We can't sell to you, if you don't supply us."

He made a grab for one of the backpacks, but Brad blocked him with his body, his eyes steely. "Hold on. Those are mine now, you've already sold them to me."

Anton gritted his teeth and gave a nod to Leon to move into position. "Actually, no sale has taken place at this point. You haven't paid us a dime and those are my packs." He threw his arm up, knocking Brad back a pace as Leon grabbed him from behind.

The driver struggled, a panicked look on his face. "Hey, you can't do that. You don't know these guys. I'll never survive."

Anton slung a pack on his back. "Then you should have done your job. How much money have you got on you?"

Leon let one arm free as the fellow tried to dig in his pocket. "How much do I owe you?"

"Lots," he snarled.

~~~~~

Back at the plane, they tucked the packages of supplies, and one backpack of product into the cargo bay. "This doesn't work," Anton said, surveying the meagre pile of supplies. "We'll have to do something else. Maybe we should fly down to Seattle, it's easier to find what we need."

Leon glanced up at the sky. "Not today," he muttered. "Too late now."

"Yeah, we'll have to stay here for the night. But we can sell the rest of the meth down there, and load up with supplies for the plant."

"Okay." Leon gave him a look. "You got pretty rough back there. I wasn't sure what your plan was."

"Well, my plan wasn't to get fleeced by the delivery guy."

"Yeah, I could see that."

"Maybe someone has stepped onto our patch over here. There must be a reason he didn't get our stuff for us. He can't seriously think he can singlehandedly rewrite our working agreement. As it is, he did okay. He'll make good money off one pack. It's quality product."

"Right." Leon turned to close the cargo hold. "I don't think it's a good idea to leave this stuff here. We should at least take the backpack with us." At Anton's nod, he pulled it out. "This way, when we sign into a hotel, it'll look like we have some luggage with us."

Anton gave a crack of laughter. "Good plan."

***

CHAPTER TWENTY-SEVEN

Kofi Aribadis parked his Mercedes in the alley and walked around the older concrete building. Comox was a fairly small town, but this Ethiopian restaurant was so much better than anything he'd found in Nanaimo or any of the other towns in the northern sections of Vancouver Island. There was a great one in Victoria, but he seldom had the time to drive that far.

Ganaye didn't like him coming here all the time, so he parked in the alley. His boss was convinced the Mercedes stood out too much and would be noted. Perhaps it would or perhaps that was paranoia talking. But Aribadis was sick of western food. The bread was thick and tasteless, the meat tough and lacking in any kind of flavour. He'd taken to cooking his own fuul, not something he would have done back home. His wife did all the meal preparation there, as was proper. He'd been surprised at the challenge of finding decent fava beans and the time it took to soak and cook them. Getting the spices right was the next chore, but he was learning. His breakfasts were improving.

The restaurant owner stood behind the till when Kofi

entered. "Hello," he called in the Oromo language. "How are you today? Haven't seen you in a while."

Kofi nodded. "Been busy," he answered in English. This language was pretty common back home, which is why he wondered at the difficulty of being understood here in Canada. "Can I order a coffee?" He slid onto the bench seat at one of the tables toward the back of the establishment. He hoped his host hadn't run out of Ethiopian coffee, as had happened once before, because the western replacement product was pathetically weak.

"Yes, sir. Home grown, as always," the host said and Kofi's stomach relaxed.

"Are you hungry?"

"Always." They grinned at each other. Ethiopians were known for being long and lean, and perpetually hungry. On the other hand, their food was low in fat and carbs.

"Lamb tibs is fresh today," the owner replied in Arabic. "Best lamb I've found in ages."

"Sounds like just what I need." Kofi settled more comfortably on the bench and lifted the strap of his carry bag off his shoulder to lay it beside him. He heaved a sigh. It was time for some decisions. There were too many signs at his work indicating change was coming, and Ethiopians had learned it was best not to ignore things like that.

Anton and Leon had departed in their plane this morning, leaving him with the mess of the fire to deal with. He was glad he'd dropped those young men at the hospital. He only hoped that his son would be taken care of in such a way, if something similar were to happen back home. He couldn't just leave them at the plant as Anton had suggested when he finally got hold of him on his phone. Kofi might be a foreigner but he wasn't inhuman.

He checked his bag to ensure his cell was turned on. He got a real earful if he wasn't available, day or night, to deal with whatever might arise.

As it was, they were now short two workers, and he'd been given no instructions, other than to ensure the plant was operating at full capacity this week. As a result, he'd talked with the two remaining workers who were understandably shaken by events. He assured them that in all the years he had worked the plant, this was the first time a fire had occurred. There were two problems with his statement. The first—he wasn't sure the workers understood much of what he said. He knew he had an accent, but surely, after all this time, they'd become accustomed to it.

The second problem— he hadn't worked for years at the plant. It had only been established for about nine months as far as he was aware, and he was the first manager. Anton had trained him, and they went from there. It wasn't likely the workers were aware how new the plant was. Neither of them was from Union Bay.

He promised a hefty bonus if they each brought in another worker to fill the vacant positions. Anton hadn't authorized the bonus, but he'd better pay it. Kofi had been given a task—keep the lab in production—and for that he needed workers.

He felt pressured to make a decision. Should he continue working for Anton Ganaye, with these clueless young workers, and wait for the roof to fall in? Or should he bolt? There were a number of ways he could leave. Yes, the car was a job perc, but nothing was stopping him from driving off Friday morning, after Ganaye picked up the bags of drugs, and then dropping the car somewhere else. Once on the mainland, he'd be free to go wherever he wanted.

On the other hand, a report to the police that a documented immigrant took off in a company car would send alarms all across the country. Would Ganaye make such a report? If not him, then Leon? Leon was not as connected to the operation, and might be more in a position to make such a complaint. He just didn't know and there was no way to find out. The other option was to leave without the vehicle. He could drive to the ferry and walk on, leaving the car here. The real question—was it time to go?

His alternate employer would rather he stay with the present organization. They had made that clear. They knew of Anton Ganaye and were monitoring the flow of drugs into their state. Having Kofi on staff here gave them an edge that they weren't willing to give up. They weren't so interested in whether Aribadis was in jeopardy or not.

The lamb tibs arrived, and he dug in. The flavour was intense and he soaked it up. The injera had a wonderful sourness to it, acting in counterpoint to the spicy meat. He tore another piece off the round flat bread and used it to scoop a mouthful of tibs. There was too much food for him to finish it all, which was good news. He'd pack it up for a second meal.

He waved for the attention of the owner. "I'll take an order of doro wot with me if you have it. Chicken would be preferred." He usually ordered a second serving of something. It meant he didn't have to wonder what to eat the next day when the plant started up again. He was as sick of the food as were the young men. Were there tears in his eyes? He must be getting melancholy, missing his family and his culture.

But not the poverty. He didn't miss that. Nor did his family now he was able to send them money. He had to keep all that in mind. *Catch 22*, as Anton Ganaye liked to say.

***

CHAPTER TWENTY-EIGHT

When Rain arrived at the Nanaimo hospital, he was directed to the burn unit on the third floor of the aging building. Walking down the corridor, walls decorated with faded paint, and scrapes from the rolling beds, he spotted a police guard at the door of a room at the far end of the hall. He showed his Dexter Winston ID. After a phone call to the Victoria detachment, he donned a mask and gown and was granted entry to the room.

The two young men lay in beds arranged side by side. They both appeared unconscious. The attending nurse informed him they were in medically induced comas—the doctor's way of letting them heal with the least amount of pain and trauma.

Rain read their names on the placard at the foot of each bed. At least now he knew the identity of the young man who had given the information to Vickers. Jason Michaels, a few pimples still on his chin, tossed restlessly against the pillow. His hair was gone, even his eyebrows were singed right off his head. The exposed skin was curled and coated with some medical cream to soothe the pain and help with healing.

"They'll both need skin grafts," the elderly nurse commented, adjusting the IV line in Jason's arm as he shifted on the mattress. "The other fellow is in more trouble. He must have had a full beard," she said. "When it burned, it took his face with it."

Rain looked over at the second bed. This young man looked in much worse shape, his flesh showing red and baked under the medical cream. He didn't move against the pillow. "Do you think you could ease back on the pain medication for tomorrow morning? I need to interview them and they obviously can't tell me anything in this condition."

The nurse shrugged. "I'll talk to the doctor," she promised.

There was a low agonised cry from the hallway, then a scuffle of feet. Rain heard the cop on duty talking softly and a woman's voice responding insistently. The door burst open and the nurse popped out of her chair. "You can't just barge in here," she stated. "This room is private. Oh." She slowly backed away from the door as a middle-aged woman staggered through, hair unbrushed and tear tracks coating her cheeks.

"Barry," the woman gasped, stopping at the first bed. She seized the young man's blistered hand. "Barry, what happened?"

"*Don't touch him, Ma'am.*" The nurse said sternly. "You could cause infection with so much damaged skin." In the midst of the noise and commotion, Barry didn't move a muscle. The nurse found a mask and gloves for the mother and waved her to a chair.

Rain slipped out of the room, and walked down the hall, his chest tight. It was too late to head home now. Sophia had sounded upset this morning, asking him for a ride to work. Why wasn't life simpler, so he'd be in the same city when she needed help? Why did things have to be so complicated?

Better to stay the night and try to talk to the young men tomorrow to see if he could glean some information. He had a feeling of deep frustration riding his shoulders. If he had been more successful in working this case, he might have cracked it before the fire started. As a result, those young men wouldn't be so badly injured.

***

CHAPTER TWENTY-NINE

After a fitful night in a roadside hotel, Rain had a quick breakfast and headed over to the hospital. Those young men couldn't stay on reduced pain killers for long in the shape they were in. The plan was to interview them as soon as possible, so the doctor could get them back on full medication and make them more comfortable. Hopefully he'd learn something useful, although he held out little expectation of that.

Sorry, he texted Sophia. *Don't know how today will unfold. I'm planning to be in town by this afternoon, but can't guarantee it.*

That's okay, she sent back. *I'm working today and the weekend is coming.*

He smiled in spite of himself. It had been quite a while since he'd had the kind of job where he actually looked forward to the weekend, knowing he'd be off work.

If all goes according to plan, he texted, *I'll be home by six tonight*. He knew he'd have to return here again shortly thereafter, but even if it meant travelling north in the middle of the night, he needed to get into Victoria to see Sophia. He had the feeling time was running out on him. He hadn't been available to drive her to work when she'd needed a lift, and another man could easily step into the breach at any moment. She was working and meeting people. It seemed inevitable she'd attract the attention of some guy.

A different cop was on guard outside the hospital room when he arrived, so he went through the process again—show ID, wait for the phone call to Victoria for approval before they let him in. He put on the mask and gown.

Inside the room, the blinds were drawn. Barry's mother was still sitting at his bedside, her head resting on the mattress beside him as they both slept. Jason Michaels was awake, his eyes gleaming dully in the morning light.

Rainier took the chair beside his bed. "Jason," he said. "My name is Dexter Winston."

Jason squinted. "Who are you?" he murmured.

"Dexter Winston. I work with the police. There's a police guard outside your door and they won't let anyone in who isn't police. Understand? You're safe here."

Jason closed his eyes a moment as a tear ran down his temple. Then he focussed on Rain's face. "Bit late, isn't it?" His voice was a mere whisper in the quiet room, barely audible above the sounds of medical equipment pumping and beeping, but Rain clearly heard the hurt and despair.

"I've just started on this case," he replied, his heart squeezing in his chest. "I was hoping you could give me some information."

Jason's eyes focussed on his face. "Like what? I already talked to the police. Not that it helped any."

"Yes, I know you did." Rain touched his shoulder in sympathy, but the young man cringed at the weight of his hand. "Sorry. I know you're in a lot of pain. But if there is anything you can tell me that would help, I'd appreciate it. Names, places, an address, anything."

"My mum," he whispered. "Look after her. These guys are deadly, and they'll go after her. I just know it."

"Okay." Rain nodded emphatically. "I'll get on that this morning. We'll keep your Mum safe. That will be our first priority. Any names you can tell me?"

Jason looked hesitant. "I don't really know names," he muttered. "The boss is called Bad Ass, probably not his real name."

"Bad Ass?" Rain suppressed a snort. "You sure that's his name? What does he look like?"

"He's a foreigner, dark skin, tall and skinny. His first name's Harry. Yeah, Harry Bad Ass. Ouch," Jason touched his ruined face gingerly with the tips of his fingers, closed his eyes and passed out.

"Jason," Rain said. "I need more information. Where do you work? If we're to shut this operation down, we need to know more." Jason didn't respond.

Rain sat in silence for a few minutes, then touched the young man's arm, but there was no reaction. This was likely all he was going to get. He glanced at Barry in the neighbouring bed, but he was comatose. His mother had come awake and was patting his shoulder and anxiously calling to the nurse, but he didn't stir.

Now Rain was left with a mother to protect, the uncooperative Detective Vickers as his police contact, and a guy named Harry Bad Ass for a suspect. He walked out of the hospital, heading for his undercover car and the Nanaimo police station.

***

CHAPTER THIRTY

Rain had seated himself across the desk from Detective Vickers as he outlined what support he needed from the detachment. The cop's Scottish accent grew stronger as the discussion became more heated. "Murdoch," he growled, "you're not the head of this investigation, I am. And you don't get to make the decisions, I do. There isn't enough in the kitty to cover protective custody for Mrs. Michaels and her son. As it is, Jason is already protected with the guard at his hospital door. But that's as far as it goes. The lad was involved in something illegal and he got his comeuppance." He slammed one hand on the desk between them. "You can take that to the bank."

"Have you been to the hospital to see what condition he's in?" Rain demanded. Getting to his feet abruptly, he squinted in an effort to disguise his reaction. "I think I'll go make a few phone calls."

Vickers sat back as his eyes narrowed. "Calls to who?" he ordered angrily. "Are you thinking of going over my head?"

"It wouldn't take much," Rain muttered as he stalked from the room. Back in his undercover car, he pulled out his cop phone and dialed Detective Ross Cullen in Victoria. After explaining the situation, he asked what actions were open to him. "Keep in mind," he repeated, "I promised Jason Michaels we'd keep his mother safe."

"I hear you, Murdoch. Give me a minute." He was put on hold and spent the next while drumming his fingers on the steering wheel. *What was the next step in this investigation?* To his mind, it was to follow the van, if it still made it's rounds and picked up the few workers who were left in Cumberland. If that didn't happen, they'd just lost their main chance at solving the case through sheer police bungling. The tension in his chest tightened with each second he waited.

Ross came back on the line. "Okay, Murdoch. I've got a safe house booked for Mrs. Michaels and a couple of guys who are heading up to get her. Does that work?"

Rain's jaw dropped. That was fast. "Has anyone phoned her?" he asked. "My bet is she'll want to stay close to her son as he heals from that fire."

"I understand. That's why Jason is being transferred to the Victoria hospital. She'll be near enough to visit as often as she wants."

"Yeah, okay. That works. Thanks Ross. You've taken care of number one on my to-do-list."

"You're welcome. What's number two on that list?"

"Well, it seems to me we have a slim chance the van will do its usual pickup on Sunday, as there are still two workers left. So I think we need to take some action. I'm fine with following it myself, if you can arrange someone to be in position to attach a tracker. I'm guessing there won't be many more chances. Losing half their work force is going to hit this operation hard." The pressure to wind the case up was rising and Rain's gut was tight from stress.

"Right. I agree with you. I understand Vickers is not cooperating on any of this."

"You got that right. Doesn't seem to know the meaning of the word." *Damn right he wasn't.* Heat rose up his chest. "There's a guy named Morse who has offered to help if needed. Do you know him?"

"Yup, good guy. But I can work that out from this end. Might take some of the weight off the Nanaimo detachment. I can have a team waiting when the van drives by Sunday night. It should be easy to trail the vehicle through town, and the driver can drop his partner off to attach a tracker when it seems expedient," Ross said.

"Okay, I like that. I'll be in position to tail the vehicle once it leaves town, but the tracker ensures we find where they go if I lose them." He took a breath. "I've got one more thing. Are you in the office this afternoon? I'd like to talk to you about another matter that I need help with."

"Sure." Ross sounded more cautious. "I'm out for a bit but should be back by three or so, and I'll be here the rest of the day."

"Sounds good. I'll see you then." Rain clicked off. Finally, he was making headway. Now if he could just manage to get home, see Sophia, and get Ross's help, he'd be a happy man.

***

CHAPTER THIRTY-ONE

Later, in Ross Cullen's cubicle of an office in the RCMP headquarters building, Rainier wound up his explanation. "His name is Anton Ganaye, he follows her and threatens her," he said. "She has a car in her name, but he's registered a lien on it so she can't get rid of it. And he claims to be an undercover cop with the RCMP."

Ross's eyes widened.

"Yeah," Rain continued. "I know you can't give me information, but I hope you can do a search and see if he is in fact a cop. If so, there's more to worry about, because then we know he's armed and has the means to find her no matter where she goes."

"Okay," Ross nodded. "I understand your concern. If he's a cop and working undercover, I won't be able to tell you a thing. However, I don't like the sound of this situation. Wait out there and give me a few minutes." He pointed to the door of his office.

Rain took a chair in the hallway and cooled his heels.

Cullen made a few phone calls and did something on his computer. Finally, the detective rose and waved him back in, his expression hard. "If this guy claimed to be with the RCMP, he was lying through his teeth. He's not a cop with us. I've got calls out to some of the local forces, but we'll have to wait for a response. It'll likely take a few days. Unfortunately, there are about five or six other police forces here on the island. Anton Ganaye might be his undercover name, so this is going to take some research. But I'm glad you brought it to my attention. I don't like it when something like this happens, and I'll happily put a stop to it once I find out what's going on."

"Great." Rain extended his hand and Cullen shook it with a forceful grip. "Let me know when you learn something. The woman is feeling pretty pressured at this point."

"I'll be in touch. Meanwhile, be careful. If he is a rogue cop, he could be dangerous."

"Yeah, I've thought of that." Rain ran a hand over the stubble on his chin. "What's the next step in this meth case?"

"Well, if you're willing to trail the van and my guys get a tracker on it, we should be in gear Sunday night, ready for action."

"Right. I'll be up there and in place." Weight lifted from Rain's shoulders. He had a whole day off, and the case was moving forward. Things were finally falling into place.

Leaving Cullen's office, he walked to the staircase and stopped in surprise. "Thea Sophia?" he croaked. She was sitting at a desk against the wall in a large open area, more desks all around, laptops in front of each occupant. Her back faced the corridor. They all wore headphones and were typing steadily on their keyboards as they listened.

Rainier backed up, trying not to attract attention and returned to Ross's cubicle. The detective was on the phone when he got there, so he waited, keeping an eye on the group at the desks. When the detective was free, he waved to get his attention. "Just as a point of interest, what are those people doing at the desks in the corner?"

Ross frowned and rose to come to the doorway and peer out. "Oh, they're transcribing audio testimony."

"And the woman at the end? How long has she worked here?"

Ross frowned and turned his head to pin him with a glare. "Who wants to know? And why?"

"Just wondering. I knew her years ago," Rain murmured. He exited in the other direction, emotion churning in his gut. It had caught him by surprise, seeing Sophia there. *What was the story?* She had some connection to the communities up island. Anton Ganaye lived in Comox and had a lot of cash but no bank accounts. The meth case was centred in that area. There was too much going on to keep it all straight in his head, but if previous experience with his partner Jeff Sanderson had taught him anything—it was to be suspicious when things didn't add up.

***

CHAPTER THIRTY-TWO

Detective Ross Cullen pulled another file forward from the pile on his desk, but his attention wasn't on it. The story Rain Murdoch had told him stuck in his craw. A man using his position as a police officer to intimidate a woman was a heinous situation. It shouldn't happen, but he knew sometimes it did. The fact this man wasn't what he'd claimed made it even more alarming.

The man was not RCMP, which ironically gave Ross some comfort. He was proud of what he did and the police force he was a part of. On the other hand, if Ganaye had been a member of this force, it would have been easier to get a handle on him and shut down his actions.

Now he was left in limbo, and would have to wait to hear back from the other forces. If Ganaye was his undercover name, it would be even more difficult to trace who he was with and his connections to the police. Ross made a couple of notes on his pad. Just a few things to check while waiting for a response from his inquiries with the other police forces on the Island.

And Vickers was being an ass. He made another note. Ross had sent Murdoch up to contribute to the investigation and Vickers was doing his best to block his access. Why bother? They hadn't been getting anywhere with the case before he arrived, why not let someone else in to do the leg work? It only made sense.

He decided to take it up with Marsh, his boss. The guy had a huge attention span and a good brain. He always found a new angle to suggest or a new contact to explore. Hopefully he'd speak to the officer in charge in Nanaimo and commandeer some cooperation from his men. John Morse was a professional, and he had obviously already reached out to make something happen.

It was also open to Ross to drag his older brother in, get his perspective and insight. Their father would want to hear about it too. Dad had retired some years back, but kept close tabs on what his sons were doing in the force.

He grinned. As the youngest cop in the family, he couldn't get away with anything. But on the other hand, his father and brother provided a lot of resources, and some useful experience to focus on this task.

He flipped open the file in front of him. Murdoch had a good mind too, which is why he'd decided to put him on this last case. He could have just let him off probation early. Murdoch probably wasn't aware of that. But Ross had decided he was needed. If that mind would allow him to make a ton of money with his own online gambling operation and invest it in commercial property, he could also use it to help the cops sort out this investigation. Then he would truly have earned his release from probation.

With a feeling of relief, Ross began to read the file notes from his assistant, Constable Dan Parker, on his next case.

***

CHAPTER THIRTY-THREE

Sophia had only been in town a couple of weeks. In Rain's opinion, she'd acted pretty fast to find a job and begin work, but more interestingly, a job with the police. Was she searching for information? What information would that be exactly? Perhaps she was after knowledge about her old boyfriend, Anton.

Rain walked a little faster, discomfort driving his steps. He didn't like to think about her trying to reach out to this guy Ganaye or possibly reconciling with him. It wasn't how things were supposed to be, damn it. He slammed the door of his truck and pulled out his cell phone.

Sophia, he texted, *I made it back to town. Do you need me to pick you up after work? What time are you off?* That way, it would be up to her to let him know where she worked.

By the time he drove to his house, there was still no reply. Obviously, she took her work ethic seriously. She answered at four-thirty. *That would be great,* she said, *I took the bus this morning, and I'm off at five.*

Where are you? he replied.

Sorry, she said. *The RCMP headquarters building.*

Right. I'll see you outside at five. Something relaxed in Rain's chest. She hadn't tried to hide where she worked. Now, all he had to do was find a way to spend some time with her.

~~~~

Rain helped himself to a second serving of Chinese food from the containers spread out on his counter and returned to his lone living room chair. Sophia had given up eating a few minutes ago, laying her half-empty plate aside.

She hardly ate enough to keep a bird alive. She was relaxed back against the sofa cushions, propping her feet on his miniscule coffee table. Her legs were perfect, slim and toned, the toenails painted purple to match her outfit. He loved the skirt, short enough to get him all excited with a nice flare at the hem. The matching blouse was a little darker in colour with the perfect amount of cleavage showing. It was enough to attract any guy's interest.

He was right to be concerned about the possibility of another man stepping in if he wasn't careful. Just knowing she worked at the police headquarters was almost a guarantee that would happen.

The way her honey-coloured hair hung down her back and curled against her chest would trigger the interest of most men. The curling ends seemed to point directly at that cleavage. And there were a lot of men coming and going in the RCMP building. He'd have to move fast if he wanted to make some headway with her.

The song on his speakers ended with a thunder of drums. "Has Toby's truck given up the ghost?" he asked.

She turned her head to give him a confused look. "What?" Then her expression cleared. "No, it just seemed a good idea to take the bus."

"Hmmm." He took a big bite of noodles from the chow mien on his plate. "You called me to ask for a ride…" He let the comment hang in the air.

Her cheeks flushed. "I know. It was a kneejerk reaction."

"To what, exactly?" He watched her expression, noting the fear that flashed there. "What, Sophia?" He dropped his plate on the coffee table beside hers. "What happened?"

A tear leaked down her cheek. "It was just— I got caught by surprise, but someone was watching the house."

"How do you mean?" Rain shifted across to the sofa and gently moved her over so he could sit beside her. "Tell me."

When he wrapped an arm around her shoulders, she shuddered and laid her head against his chest. He wondered if she could hear his heart thundering under her ear in automatic reaction to being so close to her. He wanted a kiss, but she was too upset.

"I was ready to leave for work," she continued, "when I saw a black pickup truck parked across the street. I couldn't see inside other than someone large was sitting in it. It was Anton's truck."

Rain tightened his arm and used his other hand to tilt her face up to meet his gaze. "You're sure it was him?"

She nodded. "I know it was. I recognized his truck and the licence number. The antenna is big, he installed it himself. And his rear-view mirrors are a different shape. He said all cops have those mirrors."

"Did he see you?" Rain felt like a cop himself. He wanted to interrogate her, find out everything she knew. He wanted to grab Ganaye by the throat and threaten his life if he didn't leave Sophia alone.

"No. I'm sure he didn't. There was no movement inside the truck. I left by the back way."

"The back way?" Rain envisioned the rear yard of her father's house. "How so? You couldn't get to Toby's truck that way."

"I know." She used her wrist to rub at her damp nose. "I went through the neighbour's yard to the next street. Then I caught the bus."

"Ahh. I see." Rain ran his hand over her hair. It was so soft, shining in the low light. Just the feel of it caused his cock to twitch. He hoped she didn't notice. "You must have been frightened. I'm sorry I wasn't here."

"Yes, I was scared." She glanced up at him, eyes like those of a deer caught in the headlights. "But I managed to get to work."

"Sophia, you're a wonder. Of course you managed to get to work and the next day too. Have you seen him since?"

"No, but I kept the lights off when I got home last night so he wouldn't know if anyone was home, and I peeked out the window a bunch. His truck didn't come back."

"Good." Rain ran his fingers through her hair. "I visited his house in Comox but his truck wasn't there either. I guess he was down here."

She gave him a pointed look. "You went to his house?"

He gave a decisive nod. "I wanted to get a look at him, see if I could warn him off."

"Rain, you can't do that." She gave him a searing look. "He's police. He's armed."

***

CHAPTER THIRTY-FOUR

Rain relaxed against the sofa cushions, Sophia wrapped in his arms. "I understand." He leaned his cheek against the top of her silky hair. "You know your old boyfriend's not a cop, right?"

She startled and he tightened his arm to keep her in place as she replied. "What do you mean? Of course he's a cop. He works undercover, that's why you can't find him at any police station. He's even got an undercover partner who works with him."

"What police force is he with? Is it the Royal Canadian Mounted Police or a different one?"

"No, it's the national force, the RCMP. He told me many times. He was quite upfront about it, although always cautioned me to keep it quiet. He wasn't supposed to let anyone know."

Rain leaned to plant a kiss on her flushed cheek. "I had Detective Cullen, the guy I work with, look into it. He assured me Ganaye isn't with the force. Absolutely not. He wasn't sure about the regional forces and is still doing research. But definitely not RCMP."

"What?" She looked frightened and her body shook in the curve of his arm. "How can that be? Does that mean Leon wasn't police either? They worked together on all the cases they were assigned. They both told me that."

"Well," said Rain. "They lied."

She covered her mouth with her hand. "Oh, my God. How could I be so gullible? I believed him. I believed what he told me!" She pounded her fist against her thigh, "Stupid, stupid."

Rain reached to grab her hand. "Don't say that," he murmured. "You're not stupid. He must have been pretty convincing for you to believe what he said."

More tears leaked from those bright shining eyes. "The whole thing was a lie. So what was the truth? He had money, you know." She turned to look into his face. "There was enough money to fly down to Mexico a few times. Leon didn't come with us, but they claimed he had to stay behind to keep tabs on the cases they were following. I think Leon took his own vacations when he wanted to. And there was a plane, a float plane. We flew to Vancouver a lot, sometimes to Seattle, or down the coast. It was fun." Her voice faded and she glanced down.

"What's Leon's last name?"

"Shankland," she said. "Leon Shankland."

Envy rose like a tide in his chest, suffusing his face with heat. Ganaye had enough money to take her on vacations and shopping excursions. Yet, Rain recognized this scenario. It was very much like the one he and his partner, Jeff Sanderson, had cobbled together. Lots of cash, enough to travel when and where they wanted, enough to purchase property. He should be following the money on Anton Ganaye. It would probably be much more satisfying than the meth case he was working on that never went anywhere.

He turned his head and her face was right there, too close to ignore. He laid his mouth over hers. She gave a little confused sound that just urged him on, and he deepened the kiss, running his tongue over her lips until she opened for him. Then he dove deep, tasting her, learning the textures of her tongue and mouth. He explored the edges of her teeth, as his temperature rose along with his excited cock.

He placed one hand against the side of her breast and had to lift his mouth away to pant for breath. Lord, he was lost, and he knew it. He examined her face, the rosy cheeks and eyes at half mast.

"Sophia," he said. "You can't go back to Uncle Toby's house. Anton might show up, and you're all alone out there." He poured kisses down her cheek to the soft skin of her throat. "You should stay here. There's a comfortable bed you can use, and I can sleep on the sofa." He realized he was babbling but couldn't stop himself. "I'll take you back to your father's place tomorrow early, before work, so you can get your things. You can drive my truck while I'm away, I have an undercover cop car right now. That way you'll be safe. I have to go back to Cumberland and Nanaimo soon, so I can't stay here with you."

She wrapped those slender arms around his waist. "Thank you, Rain Man," she glinted up at him. "I'd feel safer here, with someone to watch over me."

"Don't tease, Thea Sophia. I'm in no position to defend myself."

She gave a low laugh. "I'm in no position either. And I'm not teasing, I'd like to stay with you."

"Even though I'm seldom home."

"Even though," she nodded.

"Good." He kissed her again until he couldn't bear the tension and attraction. "I'm afraid I'll go too far. I don't want to frighten you." Easing back, he kept her pinned to his side as his chest heaved for breath. Having a mind of its own, his hand remained wrapped around her breast.

She blinked rapidly, her breath coming fast.

"You should go to bed. We have to be up pretty early. I'll take you to Toby's before I head up-island again. But I'll leave my truck keys here for you."

He pried himself away from her and offered his hand to help her off the sofa. "The bathroom is here," he pointed. "The bedroom is there. I'll just grab some bedding."

The sofa was damned hard and looked way too short for his length. How did Jake manage when he was here? He'd soon find out for himself how uncomfortable it had been.

***

CHAPTER THIRTY-FIVE

After a restless night's sleep, during which Rain couldn't get his mind off the thought of Sophia lying alone in his bed a few yards away, he rose to start the coffee. He was dressed and waiting to ferry her to her father's place when she emerged from his bedroom, wearing the same lovely purple blouse and skirt. He groaned inwardly. Good thing he wouldn't be home tonight. He wasn't sure he could do that again—sleep on that hard, too-short couch when she was in the next room, so close and accessible in his bed.

He handed her an insulated coffee mug and opened the door. She preceded him down the steps to his car in the parking garage at back. "You should park here," he indicated, pointing to where his truck sat in the line of vehicles. "These are the keys to the truck and the apartment door," he added, handing them to her. "I'm sorry I have to leave again today. My best hope is this case will be over soon."

She placed a soft hand on his arm. "Thank you, Rain, for

everything. I slept well last night, knowing you were there. I don't know what I would do without you." Heat flared in his chest at the feel of her hand on his arm, the thankful look in her pale blue eyes. He wished they weren't both heading off to work, but instead, could go back inside to take their clothes off and curl up together in his bed.

"You're welcome, Sophia." His gaze must have been a bit intense, because she glanced away and climbed into the car.

When he dropped her back at his apartment so she could pick up his truck, he gave her a fierce kiss. "Call the cops next time, Sophia. If there is a next time. He can't be allowed to tail you like this. It's an implied threat. You need protection."

She nodded uncertainly.

Rain headed downtown to the RCMP station, making it into the common room before Sophia arrived to take up her position on the second floor. Without the distraction, Rain hoped he would get some work done.

He could do some of this research from home, but the police system had a much longer reach and more complete information. He began on Anton Ganaye, looking for any assets he held in his own name. Now that he had information about a partner, he searched for Leon Shankland as well. He found a float plane, stationed in Union Bay, which made perfect sense if Ganaye lived up-island. There were a lot of flight plans filed that led into both Vancouver and Seattle, raising red flags in his mind around what their business might be in either city. He found two pickup trucks, one he'd already scoped belonging to Ganaye, the other to Shankland. He noted the new power supply to a building near Union Bay in Leon's name. Another issue to explore.

He recorded the new information in his little book and set up another search, wider in scope. There was information on both men from a few years ago in Saskatchewan. This data was more financial in nature—loans they had defaulted on, leases they'd signed and abandoned. The debts weren't pursued nationwide, so they still sat on someone's books somewhere. More alarming, there was a manslaughter charge brought against Ganaye a couple of years ago in Saskatoon that had been dropped for lack of evidence.

Sophia was right to be afraid. These were dangerous men.

Finally getting down to the business he was supposed to be concentrating on, Rain searched for information on Cumberland and Union Bay. What stood out in all the pages that appeared on the screen was the historical activity of Sir Robert Dunsmuir, head of an industrial and financial family on Vancouver Island in the 1800's. A Scot, Dunsmuir had been indentured to the Hudson's Bay Company to work in the coal mines at Fort Rupert, near Port Hardy, further up the coast. He soon learned all they could teach him about mining coal. Meanwhile, mines in the Cumberland area had been established, but failed to prosper until Robert Dunsmuir took them over. The community was first called Union, after the Union Coal Company that had opened the mines. Once Dunsmuir began operations, the name of the town was changed to Cumberland, although nearby Union Bay kept its name.

Rain searched further. From what he read, the coal mines were all shut down in the 1960s due to a lack of worldwide demand for the product. What had happened to all those mines since then? And exactly where were they located?

What would be simpler than to find an abandoned mine and build a meth lab? The excavation would likely be big enough to allow a dozen men to work there. They could park their vehicles inside, thereby placing them out of sight. And the young men wouldn't have a clue where they were once they'd been deposited in the mine. There wouldn't be any windows or likely even cell phone reception, although Jason Michaels had reported to police that the workers couldn't take their phones to work with them— the van driver conducted a body search on each worker before they were loaded into the vehicle.

Time was short. The task of following the van, hopefully with a tracker attached, was scheduled for tonight. Rain settled into his chair and opened up another screen, ready to conduct more detailed research, looking for the locations of the closed mines and more information on what exactly was needed to operate a meth lab.

Just as he left for up-island, he had a call from John Morse on his cop phone. Young Barry had died in hospital that morning from the burns he'd sustained in the fire.

***

CHAPTER THIRTY-SIX

Sophia's purse vibrated. She glanced around at the other workers and surreptitiously pulled her new cell phone out. The purse vibrated again. It was her old phone! Why hadn't she thrown it away? Why keep it and hang onto the connection to her past? She realized she hadn't gotten rid of it because she hadn't heard back from her father and wasn't sure if her messages were getting through on her new contact number. She had no idea what kind of reception he had in South-East Asia. Did Thailand have a lot of cell phone towers?

She put the phone away, but her purse continued to hum. Ten nervous minutes later, she left her desk for the washroom, and pulled out her old phone to examine it. The vibrations were text messages, eight of them. All from Anton, which was surprising. He hadn't reached out to her once since she'd left him months ago. The first missives pleaded with her to come back to him. She hit delete, one after the other, as revulsion churned in her stomach. The last ones were longer and consisted of threats, not nearly as conciliatory as the initial messages, but much closer to her opinion of his character. *If you don't come back, I'll find you and finish you off. Then I'll kill your father. I know where he lives.*

Tears popped into her eyes. Why couldn't he just leave her alone? She should have dumped this phone as soon as she got her new one. She felt fouled from reading his threats.

At lunch, she spent the first ten minutes deleting all the messages on the old phone. Then she deleted the contacts. Strolling down Blanshard Street toward the centre of town, she scanned the sidewalk. Soon she saw what she was looking for –a homeless man squatting in the doorway of a closed store, with his hat upside down on the sidewalk and a small sign scratched on a dirty piece of paper that read, *homeless and hungry, anything will help.*

She stopped in front of him and dug a few dollars out of her purse, dropping them into his hat. He glanced up at her, eyes clouded with fatigue and hopelessness. Then she pulled out her old phone and leaned to place it in his hat alongside the money. "There you go," she said. "It will work for about a month, then the service will be cut off. It's up to you what you do with it after that."

His face lit up like a candle. "Thank you, thank you so much. I'll guard it with my life."

She smiled. "It isn't worth your life. But I hope it's useful to you." Walking back to the building and work, her steps were infinitely lighter. *Goodbye Anton.*

Partway through the afternoon, Sophia began to have doubts about what she'd done. Perhaps she should have kept the phone and the messages so she could show them to Rain, or the police, or both now that she knew Anton wasn't police. She shrugged her shoulders at the thought she'd just made another kneejerk decision. Her life might be in danger, and Dad's too, depending on what Anton Ganaye intended to do. If Anton wasn't a cop, why did he have a revolver? She knew he had a gun, she'd seen it a few times. If he wasn't police, what was he doing all those nights away 'working'? And by giving the phone to that homeless man, had she put his life in danger, too? What a mess.

Her shoulders shook with tension. Tonight, she'd talk to Rain about it. There might be a way to retrieve those text messages even though she didn't have the phone. Rain would know. She was staying at his place again tonight, so Anton wouldn't find her at Dad's house. Her work in audio transcription was less than productive for the rest of the day.

***

CHAPTER THIRTY-SEVEN

Rain parked on the old logging road on the way out of Cumberland. This was the spot he'd identified earlier as the place to wait to follow the van. He'd rather be at home with Sophia, but he was driven to finish this case. Then he'd be free. He could make his own decisions about what he worked on or who he answered to.

He now had access to the radio frequency linked to the police system, and to the cop car in place that was destined to follow the van into the small town. He envied them. The officers in the car at least had a companion with them, someone to talk to while they waited for the action to begin. He was tired, tired of being alone and isolated. He wanted to be back at his place with Sophia. He wanted to get a life.

Just then his personal cell phone rang. He looked at the screen, recognizing the number. Chloe Bowman, his business partner. He picked it up. "Hi Chloe."

"Hi Rainier." Her voice was warm and friendly. They had come a long way in the progress of their partnership since her husband died. It was comfortable now, not frosty or stilted, suspicious.

"What's going on?" He couldn't spend much time on this conversation, he was on a stakeout.

"Okay, well, sorry to call you so late at night. I've had an offer on the back office. I thought I should check with you before I accept it. They'll take the whole space, which is good, no expenses to divide it up, and they want to rent all the parking that goes with it. What do you think?"

Rain hesitated. He'd just offered that spot to Jake to set up his PI business. On the other hand, Jake didn't have any money, and couldn't rent it right now. It wouldn't be right to put a hold on it just in case things turned out all right on that front.

"What kind of company is it?" he stalled. "Are they already in business in town and just want a bigger space or a second location?"

"No, that's the thing. They have a shop in Seattle, and are thinking of breaking into the Canadian market. They do corporate employment, find employees for large companies."

"Sounds legitimate," he said.

"I think they are. I had a look at their website, it looks good. They won't be moving in for a few months, so no rush. I just thought given we own the place jointly, we should agree on who our tenants are going to be."

"Thanks for that, Chloe. Do what you think is best. I don't know these guys, but that space has been empty for a long time. It would be good to have it rented out."

"Okay, thanks Rainier. I'll go ahead with the paperwork." She hung up.

Rain dropped his phone in the cup holder and pondered this new development. There were lots of ways Jake could set up shop in Victoria. Given that Rain's apartment was too small now, he'd get a house for him and Sophia and they could run a business out of that space once it was vacant. Jake could live in the apartment, as well. It would work. He'd make it work. He put it out of his mind to concentrate on tonight's job.

As he waited, he ruminated on the information gathered so far. He had two names from Jason Michaels— Harry Bad Ass and Jerry. When Jason first said *Bad Ass,* Rain's reaction had been to laugh, which, luckily, he'd managed to suppress. After all, Jason was lying on a hospital bed with burns over half his face and body. But at the same time, the name triggered something in his memory. Now he ran it round and round in his mind. What could Bad Ass mean? Or more to the point, what did it sound like?

He pulled his notebook from his shirt pocket and flipped on the tiny light attached to his key chain. He paged through, arriving at the notes taken when he was identifying the various vehicles going in and out of Cumberland on the camera recordings. Then he found the owners' names.

There it was, right there in front of him. Kofi Aribadis, the name of the owner of the dented grey Mercedes that had been up and down the road more than a few times, drawing Rain's attention.

Could that sound like Bad Ass to a couple of high school dropouts who worked for cash? Probably, especially if the young men weren't familiar with foreign names. And what had Jason said? Bad Ass was the boss, and he looked foreign. Rain tried to remember the driver's licence photo connected to Aribadis. He'd have to look it up when he got home, but the feeling of a breakthrough was strong in his gut. He switched the light off.

The van showed up on the road right on schedule, travelling at a sedate speed into downtown Cumberland and stopping at the first house. From the chatter on the radio, the cop car stopped behind the van, let a man out, and carried on to pass the vehicle. No one knew how many workers were on schedule to be picked up and they didn't want to miss their one and only chance to attach a tracker.

According to the police driver, he slowly circled the block and loaded his guy back into the cop car once the device was in place.

Rain let out a pent-up breath and started his car. Surveillance reported the vehicle collected three workers, so the boss had obviously been recruiting in the last few days, given that two of his workers had been hospitalized, and there'd reportedly only been four in the first place.

Soon the van headlights approached through the dark. Rain made sure his lights were out and waited patiently until the vehicle was well past his hidden spot before pulling out behind it. He took his time, delaying until he saw a curve in the road to block the view of his vehicle before turning his headlights back on.

This seemed like simplicity itself. It was about time they got moving on this case. Even if he lost sight of his target, they had the tracker in place to lead them to its final destination. By this time tomorrow, they should know exactly where these workers were taken.

It began to drizzle. Rain held back, wipers slowly slapping across his windshield. He didn't want to alarm the van driver, whose speed was moderate and steady. Obviously, Jerry was careful to do nothing to draw attention to his vehicle.

Partway to the Union Bay junction, Rain caught headlights in his rear-view mirror, distant at first but quickly approaching. The lights loomed fast, then filled his car with their glare. He pulled slightly to the right to allow this guy to get by if he couldn't wait for a passing lane.

There was the roar of an engine, then a tremendous crash that alarmed his brain and numbed his hearing in equal measure. Rain was thrown back against the seat to the sound of glass splintering around him, then bounced forward again, hitting the steering wheel as a vehicle thundered by on his left. The seatbelt yanked on his shoulder, dislocating something— he recognized the sensation from his hockey days. His forehead smashed against the windshield, breaking the skin. He must have passed out for a minute.

The next thing he became aware of, he was hanging upside down in his seatbelt, his car sliding down a hill until it came to rest lying on its roof in the ditch. His engine was still running, the vehicle rocking from the force of the wheels racing in the air above his head. Something warm and wet was running up his forehead into his hair.

He tried to orient himself, but when he grabbed for the ignition key, his hand moved in the wrong direction. Counter-intuitive as it seemed, he had to reach up to find the key and turn the engine off. The ensuing silence was deafening. All he was aware of was his breath bellowing in his chest as pain spread throughout his body.

Sometime later, although Rain had no idea how long it had been, an ambulance came barreling down the road, sirens shrieking, and stopped on the verge above his location. By this time, Rain had detached his seatbelt and collapsed onto the roof of the vehicle.

He had pain everywhere. A pair of medics slid into the ditch and hammered on his window. He fumbled with the door handle, tugging to unlock it as two cops joined the troop working to help extract him, carefully sliding him onto a stretcher and strapping him down. Then they toted him up the slippery slope to the road in the cool darkness.

***

CHAPTER THIRTY-EIGHT

When Rain woke the next morning, he blinked to bring his location into focus. He was having trouble seeing clearly. Clad in a hospital gown, he was lying on an uncomfortable bed with sidebars to keep him from falling out, which gave him a clue as to where he was. His head ached, he was wearing a neck brace, and his shoulder burned. A plastic bag full of liquid hung on a pole beside the bed and he had an IV shoved into his arm. He shifted and it triggered more aches and pains in various parts of his body.

A nurse quietly walked into the room. When she saw he was awake, she stuck a thermometer into his mouth which effectively stopped the flow of questions he'd been about to spout. She secured a little clip on the end of his finger and adjusted the drip feed from the IV bag, then removed the thermometer.

Rain grinned even though his face hurt. "Can I ask my questions now?"

She smiled. "Let me tell you what I know, then you're welcome to ask away. You arrived here, unconscious, about ten last night. The doctor put a few stitches in your forehead to close the gash and stop the bleeding. Then he popped your shoulder back into its socket."

As she paused, Rain moved his arm to see how much motion he had. Not too bad, and the pain was bearable.

"He said not to move it today. We'll be putting a tension bandage on your arm and shoulder."

Rain shrugged. He'd had dislocated joints before and always found it best to get them into motion as early as possible. Gently of course. It speeded up the healing process. But he nodded in agreement. He didn't want to be here any longer than necessary.

"Okay, what else?" he asked. "What's this for?" He pointed at the IV.

"Mostly for fluids, and pain meds. We didn't know how long before you regained consciousness."

"So, does that mean we can take it out now?" He looked up at her hopefully.

She laughed. "I'll check."

As she turned to go, he called after her. "I'd like to be released this morning."

"Don't know about that," she called over her shoulder as she left the room, disappearing from view.

A guy in a lab coat soon arrived and removed the IV, sticking a bandage over the hole in his arm. Rain swung his legs to the side, and grabbing the frame of the bed, lowered his feet to the floor.

"Go slow," the guy admonished. "Use the crutches."

"I just need to get to the bathroom. My shoulder's too sore for the crutches."

"Right." Lab coat came around and seized his uninjured arm, helping to lever him upright. Rain staggered toward the facilities, grabbing his gown closed at the back to avoid alarming the staff. He closed the door but didn't lock it, on the attendant's advice. No need to bash the door in if he passed out in here. He completed his business and moved slowly across the floor to wash his hands which were covered in blood and dirt.

As he scrubbed, he glanced in the mirror. He looked like a poster from a horror movie. There was a large white bandage glued to the middle of his forehead. Dried blood streaked his hair and face. One eye was swollen and purple, which helped explain why his eyesight was so poor.

Maybe he wasn't going to get out of here this morning after all. He brushed the flakes of blood out of his hair with his fingers as best he could, found a washcloth and cleaned his face and neck, then staggered back to bed, barely making it before he collapsed into a deep sleep.

Later that morning he called Sophia, but she didn't answer. Then he began texting her new number to let her know he'd been unavoidably delayed, something she would have already figured out from the fact he didn't make it home last night. He finally received a reply just before he was released from hospital.

At least now he knew she was okay and had gone to work. Nothing dire had occurred since his departure the day before. Somewhat mollified, he limped into the Nanaimo police station.

His neck was still in a brace, but he'd given up the crutches at the hospital. It was no surprise Vickers was not available, but the officer at the desk informed him Morse was in.

A quick phone call and Morse emerged from the common room to escort him back. "Murdoch," he said, "good to see you up and about. I heard the details of the accident this morning when I reported to work."

"Okay." Rain sat down with a relieved sigh at one of the desks. "What did you hear? Because I'm not sure what happened last night."

"From what I was told," Morse said, "you were tailing the van when you were rear-ended into the ditch."

"Right. I knew that. What happened afterward? Did the tracker on the van work? Any information on the vehicle that nailed me? I just want to wind this thing up and be done with it."

"Yeah, me too." Morse pursed his mouth. "The two cops in the undercover car behind you said they were passed by a speeding black pickup, no other information. Their dashcam was operational, of course, but the truck lights were out. The picture caught two digits of the licence plate. The guy hit you, then took off. They only knew you were in the ditch because your headlights were still on. They put in the call for an ambulance."

"Good of them." Rain glanced down. "A black pickup– and it took off fast." He had a strong feeling he was the intended target in that 'accident' last night. It would be worth looking into.

He glanced at Morse. "The pain killers they've pumped into me are starting to wear off, so I need to find a pharmacy fast. Tell me about the tracker."

"Okay." Morse straightened in his chair. "The tracker is live, but we still don't know where the van is parked. When we get close, the feed starts to go round in circles. We're organizing an all-out search to find it, a full crew of guys, search dogs, the works. We have the general area figured out. It's in Union Bay, or nearby. Just can't find it specifically."

"I'd like to be in on that." Rain thumped the table for emphasis, then frowned as his head began to pound.

"Forget it." Morse stood. "You're too beat up to take part. Go home and recuperate, you don't look so good. I'll keep you posted."

"Yeah, I know you will. Listen, thanks for replacing my car. The guy who delivered it found me at the hospital and gave me the keys."

Morse gave a short nod, a curve to his lips that was almost a smile.

"I want to be there for the search," Rain insisted, "even if I can't take part. I have some ideas about where this place might be, and I want to make sure nothing gets overlooked, that we find what we're looking for this time."

Morse shrugged. "Okay, I'll let you know what the plan is once we've got it finalized. If you get here by noon on the day selected, you can ride with me. You could stay in the car and monitor the radio frequencies if you can manage it.

That would actually be a big help."

"Good." Rain stood and shook hands. "Thanks John, I appreciate it. My job is to finish this case so I can be released from my conditions. That's what I need to happen."

"I know." Morse gave him a piercing look. "I've seen your file. If we sort this out soon, it will all be on you. You've been the lifeblood of this investigation so far, and I'll put that in writing if it's needed."

Rain nodded and limped out. At least someone had his back. It was a relief to know Morse was on his team, even if Vickers wouldn't cooperate.

When he drove down the street in Comox, he noted Anton Ganaye's black truck wasn't there. Yes, this would definitely bear looking into. The encounter on the road out of Cumberland had been no accident.

There was a older grey Mercedes parked at the curb in front of Ganaye's house. The licence number was the same as on the car that Aribadis drove, he was sure. Rainier pulled over down the block and checked his duffel bag for another tracker. Walking back, he attached it to the bumper of the grey car and took another photo of the licence plate. Something had to give here.

The drive home seemed to take forever. Rain stopped at the edge of town to drop his pain prescription at a pharmacy and wait for it to be filled. He managed to down two pills on a dry swallow, and kept driving, anxious to reach his flat. Pulling round the back of the house, he noticed the parking spot for his truck was empty. Sophia must still be at work, although it was getting late.

Grabbing his duffel, he stumbled up the back steps and unlocked the door. "Hello," he called, but, as expected, the place was empty. His whole body ached. Scratching beneath the neck brace, he ran the cold water in the kitchen and gulped a glass full along with another painkiller. He sat down heavily on the sofa and unlaced his boots. It felt like a week instead of just a day and a half since he'd left to go up-island to follow the van.

Shrugging out of his shirt and jeans he staggered into the bedroom and collapsed on the bed. Everything hurt. Those pain pills should have kicked in by now. He rolled to his side, then pried off the neck brace. There was no way to get comfortable with it strapped around his neck.

Head buried in the pillow, he drew a deep breath. The bedding smelled like Sophia. He smiled as a feeling of comfort and pleasure flooded his chest.

***

CHAPTER THIRTY-NINE

Sophia pulled Rain's truck around the side of his house and into the designated spot. There was a car in his second space but it was a different vehicle than the one he'd been driving yesterday. She yawned and glanced at the back of the building. No lights on in Rain's suite. Maybe someone else was using his parking spot.

She climbed out, taking her purse and the bag of groceries with her. She pushed her shoulder into the truck door to close it, then walked across the yard toward the back steps.

She hadn't slept well last night, tired of all the upheaval in her life. Staying at Dad's by herself had been nerve-wracking enough and having Anton show up made it doubly so. Then she'd moved to Rain's place. But it was still strange accommodations for her, and without Rain there, she'd noticed a lot of creaks and groans that seemed different from the first night, causing her to shudder alone in the dark. She finally got up and found herself a butcher knife from the kitchen to take to bed with her.

She'd been waiting for Rainier to come home, but that never happened either. If Rain was back now, she was glad she'd remembered to return the knife to its drawer. It would be embarrassing if he was to discover she was still a little kid at heart.

Shifting her packages to one arm, she struggled with the key, finally getting it fitted into the lock. It turned with ease. Rain told her he used graphite to keep the old locks working in the dated structure. So like Rain to take care of all the details, ensuring the functionality of the place. It had been such a relief to hear from him late this morning. He'd explained he'd been delayed because his car was damaged in a minor accident, but he expected to be back today some time.

She walked in and placed everything on the kitchen counter. It was very quiet, perhaps he wasn't home after all. She took her shoes off by the door and hung her jacket on the hook, then tiptoed into the living room. Rain's boots were scattered in front of the sofa, a shirt and dingy pair of jeans thrown over the back. The relief was overwhelming. She kicked at the scuffed boot nearest her, and grabbed the clothing off the cushions. He was back. She released the breath she hadn't been aware of holding.

She peered through the bedroom door. He was lying on the bed on his side, snoring softly. The blanket was shoved to his waist and a neck-brace tossed on the floor. Tiptoeing in, she picked up the brace and noted the dried blood inside the padded circle. There were purple bruises rising on the skin of his arms and shoulders. It had been no minor accident.

Tears blurred her vision as she gently pulled the sheet up

to cover him. Then she walked softly back to the kitchen. Turning on the oven, Sophia unpacked the groceries and began to prepare dinner. Rain would probably be hungry when he woke. He was a Murdoch, after all.

***

CHAPTER FORTY

When the timer dinged, Sophia pulled the pan of breaded chicken breasts from the oven and set it on the stovetop. Then she eased the lower oven rack forward and plucked out the baked potatoes. Salad was ready and waiting on the counter, with bowls and plates laid out along with the cutlery needed.

She closed the oven door and turned it off, pausing. Should she wake Rain? She'd checked on him a couple of times and noticed he hadn't moved from the position he'd been in when she first laid eyes on him. Wouldn't it be better if he moved around a bit? What if he wasn't sleeping, but had passed out in there? Although the steady snoring was probably a strong indication that wasn't the case.

She heard a rustling noise and hurried into the living room to find Rain leaning unsteadily in the bedroom doorway. He had on his boxers, but his upper body was covered in emerging bruises, the colours ranging from red to blue and purple. Her chest tightened in alarm at the startling sight. The white bandage on his forehead didn't help.

"Sophia, is that you? What smells so good?"

She moved forward slowly, a smile forming on her mouth. "I was just debating whether to wake you or let you sleep," she said.

"Whoa. No contest. You always wake a Murdoch when the food's ready." He frowned as if his head hurt. "That is dinner I smell, isn't it?"

"Yes." Sophia eased forward, wrapping a supportive arm carefully around his bruised ribs. "And it's all ready for you. Come and sit at the table."

"Careful, I'm in a bit of pain." He stalled a minute, then stepped out of her grip. "Let me put a shirt on."

"I'll get it." Sophia opened his closet. "I think this one." She pulled a short-sleeved Hawaiian print shirt from the hanger and held it so he could slip his arms in. "I like the pattern."

Rain staggered and put one hand against the wall for support. "You like this one, eh? Are you aiming for a trip to the Hawaiian Islands?"

She grinned up at him impudently. "Why don't you come and sit down before you fall down? You're too heavy for me to lift."

Rain released a deep breath and rested his arm around her shoulders. "I'll just lean on you, if that's okay. I'm a little unsteady."

Slowly, they made their way into the kitchen and Sophia paused by the nearest chair at the small table. "Sit here," she said. "I'll serve us dinner."

Rain gazed appreciatively at the plate she placed in front of him as his stomach gave a loud growl.

Sophia laughed. "Did you mention you were hungry?"

"No, but I forgot to eat today, I was busy."

"Yes, so I see." She brought her own plate to the table and fetched butter, sour cream, salt and pepper. "Eat up, so you can tell me what really happened."

Rain already had a bite of chicken in his mouth. "Mmmm," he murmured around it. "This is great. No one has ever cooked anything here before." He waved vaguely at the ancient stove. "At least not since I moved in. I've done a few things, like macaroni and cheese, but nothing as tasty as this. You're so good to me, Sophia. Is there dessert?" he asked hopefully.

"Maybe. if you're a good boy and clean your plate," she teased, as pleasure eased through her breast at his compliment. "Now quit stalling, and tell me what happened."

He gave her a pointed look. "I told you in my text message."

She shook her head. "You said there'd been a small accident. I've seen your bruises. Your chest has a purple mark in the centre about the size of a dinner plate."

"The steering wheel," he muttered.

"Someone hit you with a steering wheel?"

He snorted, and wolfed down a huge bite of potato. "No, someone hit me with a truck." His face went blank at her gasp. "See, that's why I didn't want to tell you. You'd get all worried or something."

"Of course, I'd worry. You're a mess. Tell me the rest."

"Okay." As Rain explained the events of the night before, Sophia battled with a feeling of déjà vu. She'd been afraid he would get hurt if he got involved with her, yet this had to do with the police case he was working on, not Anton Ganaye. Maybe she wasn't responsible after all. Maybe her old boyfriend had nothing to do with it.

"There." Rain gestured at his empty plate. "I ate my dinner, like a good boy. It was absolutely delicious. Where's dessert?"

She had to laugh at the impish expression on his face, even though the bruises on his jaw had turned darker as he ate.

She pulled open a cupboard door. "It's cake," she said. "I baked it last night, thinking you would be home."

His blue eyes darkened as he looked into hers. "I'm sorry. I expected to be home, I planned to be here."

"I know." She waved that away with her hand. "The cake is still here, untouched."

His gaze sharpened as he watched her bring it to the table. "What kind?"

"Chocolate, of course."

He laughed, a rusty sound that swept over her like the run of fingers across her skin, ending at her nipples. She turned away quickly in an attempt to hide her reaction, searching for a clean knife in the drawer. "I'll cut you a piece, and the coffee is ready."

"Coffee would be great. I can get it." He made to get up and winced from the effort.

"You sit still, I'll pour. Cream, no sugar, right?"

"You don't have to wait on me," he murmured. "You already did all the cooking."

Sophia gave him her best frown, which elicited a saucy grin. "Okay, Miss I'm-In-Charge," he said, relaxing into his chair. "I know when to back off."

"Sure you do," she replied. "Is it when you can hardly stand? Or when you've been in a car accident?"

"That's the thing." He frowned into the coffee cup she placed in front of him. "I don't think it was an accident."

***

CHAPTER FORTY-ONE

"We should sort out how we'll sleep tonight," Rain said, standing in the bedroom doorway. "It's going to be tough, because as your host I can't let you sleep on the sofa. Besides, its hard as a board and extremely uncomfortable."

Sophia gave a little laugh and he smiled into her beautiful pale blue eyes. "On the other hand," he added, "I'm too beat up to sleep on the sofa. I'm not sure what other options are open."

He watched her gaze dart to the unmade bed as her lips turned up in a smile. "Good question," she said. "What other options are there? I could go back to Dad's house."

Rain pulled her gently against his frame as his shoulder shot an agony of objections. "Forget it. That's not going to happen. Too dangerous."

"Well, then. I don't know," she said, staring into his eyes. Gently, she placed her hands on his shoulders. "I wouldn't want you to get hurt."

"No, we'll have to take great care that doesn't happen." He

focussed on her lush mouth, the full bottom lip calling to him. Slowly, giving her time to pull back, he lowered his head and laid his mouth over hers. The sense of connection was instantaneous. She nestled against him, where she fit perfectly. Finally, getting somewhere with Thea Sophia. He angled his head to deepen the kiss and felt a stab of pain in his neck. He grunted, but waited it out and as the sensation eased, he plunged his tongue into her mouth. Just where he wanted to be. It was a long time before he raised his aching head.

"Rain?" Her soft voice soothed all the painful spots in his body. "Are you all right?"

"I'm just fine," he said with satisfaction, "but pretty tired. Must be time for bed. You get ready first. I'll read my email." He settled down at his desk in the corner and opened up his laptop. There had been a few items during the day from Ross that showed up on his phone and required his attention. No time like the present. He actually felt better than when he first woke. He'd been hungry and Sophia had provided the perfect meal to kick up his energy levels.

He heard the shower go on in the bathroom, and paused, his gaze riveted to the door. He'd give just about anything to be in there with her. Maybe not tonight, but when he was feeling stronger.

The emails quickly downloaded. Three from Ross Cullen, one from John Morse reporting that the search day had finally been scheduled. Rain read it with relief, determined to be feeling well enough in a few days to play his part in the race to find the van. He was committed to seeing this thing through and putting it to bed.

Thinking of which, he glanced up as Sophia left the bathroom, padding in bare feet into the bedroom. Her hair was damp and combed back from her forehead, and she wore the same robe she'd had on the first day he found her at Uncle Toby's when she opened the door to his knock. The emerald green of the fabric made her skin look smooth and warm. He sincerely hoped she had a nightgown to wear, or, even in his present condition, he wouldn't get much sleep.

He glared at the laptop screen. Just one more task to complete. He pulled up the contact information for the vehicle yards and car wreckers he'd often consulted while looking for a replacement car in the old days when he changed vehicles so frequently. He described a black pickup truck, a large custom antenna and special rear-view mirrors with the front end badly crunched in a probable rear-ender. Had any of them recently received such a vehicle? He was sure someone out there knew something and these guys had worked with him in the past.

Now his head hurt like crazy and his shoulder was giving him hell. Time for some more pain pills. He staggered off to the bathroom, downed the pills and stumbled into the shower. Feeling cleaner, he wrapped a towel around his waist and managed to hobble back to the bedroom. The light was out, but he made out the shape of Sophia's body under the covers on the other side of the mattress. He barely managed to pull on a clean pair of underwear before collapsing into bed. As he succumbed to unconsciousness, he wrestled with the disappointment that he finally had Sophia in his bed, and he was in no condition to do anything about it.

Rain woke early to a body full of pain and a driving need to get to the bathroom to relieve himself. He downed a few more painkillers, drinking from the glass on his night table. Light was just beginning to show around the window blinds and his clock said quarter after five. He rolled over and bumped into a body under the covers. Sophia! He hadn't forgotten she was there, but had been sunk in a well of unconsciousness all night.

His hand landed gently on her hip as he realized she was facing away from him. He shuffled softly forward, aligning his body with hers, and wrapped one arm around her waist. Her flimsy nightgown clung to his fingers. She snuffled into the pillow and shifted her legs.

He relaxed slowly into the mattress, waiting for the pain medication to kick in. He was positive he'd feel a whole lot better in a few minutes. Once his body stopped protesting, he eased out of the sheets, silently lowering his feet to the floor.

In the bathroom, he relieved himself and glanced in the mirror. His face looked pretty rough. Peeling the bandage off his forehead, he examined the gash. Better. The doctor had done a good job with the stitches, and without the Band-Aid he looked less like the walking dead. When he pulled his bangs forward, the mark was barely visible. However, the scruff on his jaw would definitely put paid to any action he was hoping to initiate in bed. He lathered his face and conducted a close shave, hoping Sophia was still sleeping.

He adjusted his boxers around the semi-erection he'd been sporting all night, and opened the bathroom door. Sophia was lying exactly the way he had left her. He quietly walked back to bed, and crept beneath the sheet, sliding over to press his chest against her back. He closed his eyes, drawing in a deep breath along with the scent of woman. His chest expanded in pleasure as he drifted off.

***

CHAPTER FORTY-TWO

When Sophia woke, she was overly warm. Ripples of pleasure formed in her tummy as she realized a large hand was wrapped around her breast. There was no question in her mind whose hand it was. Rain had slept restlessly, rising from the bed several times in the night. She'd been worried about him, but when she roused and asked how he was, he just muttered something about *go back to sleep*. She shifted under the weight of his arm and felt a slow line of little kisses as they were planted on the back of her neck.

She smiled to herself, tugging her nightie down from where it was tangled around her hips. "Rain?"

"That's me," he said, his morning voice rough. "How did you sleep?"

She rolled to face him, causing his hand to lose its grip on her breast. He shifted to settle it on her belly, as she registered rising excitement beneath his touch. "Pretty well. You got up a few times. How do you feel now?"

"I only got up once, I think, to take pain meds. I feel good." He grinned.

She giggled, examining his face. The purple around his

eye was less noticeable, and the white patch was gone from his forehead. She pushed his hair back to examine the stitches. "You don't look like you feel good. Although your face is a bit better. Not as swollen." She shifted. "Cover your eyes, I have to get up to use the bathroom."

"Okay, if you insist. But I'd rather..."

"Rain!" She shuffled across and grabbed her housecoat from the chair beside the bed, pushing her arms into the sleeves. "There, now I'm decent."

"You looked pretty decent before," he murmured.

"How do you know? Were you looking?" she demanded. Of course he was looking. Why would she think otherwise? This was Rain Man she was dealing with.

He snorted. "You weren't supposed to hear that."

She walked toward the bathroom across the creaky floorboards. His place was old but she liked it—the huge wooden beams in the ceilings, the lath and plaster walls. Rain had pointed out all the details when she'd first arrived. The bathroom was a modern addition to the original structure. She was quite sure there had been an outhouse in the back yard when it was first built, kind of like back home on the farm when she was small.

She brushed her hair and fluffed it a bit. It had been wet when she went to bed and appeared flat on one side. She'd simply been too tired to blow it dry. It seemed odd that she'd slept with Rainier Murdoch in his bed, yet nothing had happened between them. She snickered. Even if he'd intended something to happen, he was in no condition to make love to her.

When she emerged from the bathroom, Rain was leaning in the doorway of the bedroom, a shirt thrown over his shoulders. "Come back to bed," he said. "We need to talk." He grinned, then put his hand to the side of his face in obvious pain.

Sophia rolled her eyes. "We need to talk in bed?"

"Yeah." He dropped his hand and put on a hangdog expression. "I'm still pretty beat up. I have to rest."

"Oh, okay." She nodded. That much was definitely true. She took his arm to help him back to his side of the bed.

"Do you work today?" he asked.

"No, I have a day off. We all do."

"Oh, I remember now. You already told me. I kind of lost track." He patted the sheet beside him. "Crawl in here and cuddle with me. I'm feeling pretty low."

"Poor Rain," she whispered, circling the bed and sliding under the covers. "You've been beat up."

"Yeah, I have." He carefully raised his good arm and wrapped it around her as she drew near, urging her closer to his side.

She snuggled against him, resting her palm in the wedge of dark hair in the centre of his hard chest. "Although, I think I've seen you this battered before, when you were still playing hockey."

She felt his chuckle vibrate under her hand. "Yup," he murmured. "Can't say this is new. Except the whiplash was a bit of a surprise. "

"Have they caught the guy who did it to you?"

He sobered quickly as he stared into her eyes. The startling intense blue always took her by surprise. "Not yet. Not that I know of."

She grew uncomfortable under his gaze and glanced away. "What do we have to talk about?"

"Oh, that. Well, a few things. First, I need some sympathy. A few kisses to ease my pain."

She giggled and looked back at him. "You said you were feeling better. *Good* was the word you used."

"Well, that was because you were lying in bed right next to me. Then you left. I felt abandoned, and I'm just starting to recover." He tightened his arm.

"Starting to recover?" She shifted against his chest, leaning up on one elbow and placing her mouth over his. She felt the connection instantly. Rain had always been her hero, and now he needed her help. He pressed his lips to hers, his tongue seeking entry and exploring the edges of her teeth. She opened her mouth wider to gulp some air and he took advantage, rolling over and pressing her down against the pillow as he deepened the kiss.

The feel of his lips on hers was mesmerizing and she'd kind of forgotten where she was when he suddenly pulled back with a low groan. "*Damn.*" He collapsed on his back against the headboard, blowing out a breath in frustration. "I can't do this. My shoulder gets in a wringer every time I move. *Shit.*"

***

178

CHAPTER FORTY-THREE

Sophia tried not to laugh at his disappointed look. She pulled his shirt aside and pressed her mouth against his chest. "I think you should take this off," she said, tapping the three buttons that remained fastened.

"Oh, good idea." Rain fumbled with the buttons and tugged the shirt off one arm. She moved to help, slowly easing it from the swollen shoulder.

"That's better, now lie back."

"Okay." He relaxed against his pillow, one hand fingering the hem of her nightie. "I think you should take that off, too."

"Huh. I'll think about it," she said.

He looked crestfallen.

"Take it easy, Rain Man." She grinned and crawled forward on her knees until she hovered over his reclining body. Then she placed both hands on his chest, bracing herself, careful to avoid the worst bruising. Bending her head, she kissed him.

"Ahhh." He breathed out into her mouth as both hands rose to grab her around the hips and pull her over him. "Perfect," he said, "Sophia, you're just perfect." She shut him up with her tongue, and he dove into the kiss, pulling her down to lie on his chest as his mouth worked on hers.

After a moment, she realized his hands were worming their way under her nightie, one placed at the small of her back to hold her against him, the other tunnelling its way between her legs. She pulled back. "Rain?"

"Come here," he said. "This won't hurt, I promise." Just then his fingers found their target. She felt a responsive clenching of inner muscles that caught her off guard. His fingertips continued to smooth her tender flesh, causing heat to flood her belly and lower.

Rain lifted his hips to rub himself against her. She pulled back and wrapped her fingers around his erection through his boxers. He groaned. "Take off that nightie. I need to see you."

"Haven't decided yet," she said and squeezed a little harder.

He grunted and grabbed her wrist. "Sweetheart, you'll finish me before we get started."

She relaxed her hand and he grinned. "That's better. I love you, Thea Sophia."

Pleasure flowed like a river beneath her breast. She'd loved him for so long, following along in his wake as they grew up. "It's Sophia now," she murmured, distracted.

"I know," he said, "but I've always called you Thea Sophia. I promise to work on changing my ways." Rain's hand shifted. "Try this." He tugged the hem of her nightie upward and slowly raised it over her head. "There we go." Okay, so she had decided.

His gaze was riveted to her breasts and she thought about folding her arms across her chest to protect them from his gaze. But this was Rainier, the man she'd been fascinated with forever. She finally had his attention. She leaned forward, pressing her nipples against his chest.

"Holy." He slid one hand up her back to anchor her and lifted his hips to grind himself against her where she was splayed across him. He tugged at the waistband of his boxers and slid them down his hips.

His erection touched her at her most vulnerable spot and she froze. Glancing up, she met his gaze. "I'm on the pill," she said.

He nodded. "I know. I saw the package in the bathroom." He shifted his hips and nudged himself upward so the tip of his penis dipped inside her. The sensation was electrifying. She rose onto her knees, wrapped her fingers around him to hold him in the right spot and slowly lowered herself.

Rain was breathing like a freight train, which matched her thundering breath perfectly. When he was finally seated inside her, she leaned forward. He placed both arms around her and held her tight, rocking softly to massage her tender inner tissue. Then he kissed her and jackknifed upward at the same time, so that she couldn't catch her breath.

The sensations were overwhelming. She lost focus, just concentrating on the rising excitement within. "Rain," she murmured. "Do that again."

"Oh, I will, sweetheart. I will." He seized her hips and began a steady penetration that touched the perfect inner spot and sent her into orgasm. He followed her over the edge.

***

CHAPTER FORTY-FOUR

Anton rose early, there was a lot to organize. He sat at his table and grabbed a sheet of paper. Shifting on his chair, he checked to ensure he had a clear view of the street in front of the house, in case any unexpected, and unwelcome, visitors should show up.

There was a lot on his mind—Leon, the fire in the plant, the death at the hospital of one of his workers, the truck. He leaned forward and began today's list

Item one – take care of transportation. He'd already gotten rid of his truck. Now all he had to do was register the Mercedes in his name. He'd ordered Aribadis to bring his car over and leave it here. When he arrived, Anton got his manager to sign the papers transferring ownership. That done, all he had to do was register the vehicle in his own name. Aribadis lived close enough to the plant to walk to work, anyway. He didn't really need the car.

Item two — the fire. In his mind, this was the time to shut

down the whole operation. He couldn't delay any longer. All lines led back to him, and the cops must be closing in, although he hadn't seen any signs of that, other than the police guard in the hospital. Even the guard was gone now. One patient died, and the other left. He certainly hadn't returned to his home in Cumberland, Anton had checked. But the death would bring the police down on them for sure. They couldn't ignore the situation now. This was the last batch of meth to be manufactured— the workers would go home and never return.

Item three—Leon. It was time to divorce his partner. Leon hadn't made a positive contribution for some time. It was over. When the plant went, so would Leon. Anton was determined.

Item four—make plans for his future. Where should he go from here? He had the Mercedes and the plane. But he couldn't take both with him, so he'd sell the car and fly out. A float plane limited where he'd end up. Anywhere along the west coast would do, and there were a lot of inland lakes that were isolated and large enough to operate the plane from. The possibilities were huge. He had the equipment to set up a meth lab, and he had the know-how. He had established suppliers and buyers. All he needed was another site to operate from. Easy peasy, as they say.

He examined his list for next steps, folded the paper and put it in his pocket. Picking up his phone, he called a used car dealer to start the ball rolling on the sale of his car.

~~~~

Rain woke when Sophia slid out of his arms. He couldn't believe he'd fallen asleep again. Seemed like he'd been dozing almost steadily since he made it back home yesterday afternoon.

"Where are you going?" he murmured, stretching his back. He felt terrific. He watched her naked butt disappear beneath the nightie as she shrugged it over her head.

"I'm going to make breakfast, or lunch, depending on what I feel like when I get to the kitchen."

"Is it that late?" He glanced at his clock which showed well past noon. "Eggs and bacon would be good," he called, then grinned at the glare she shot him. "Come here and let's talk about it."

She snickered, grabbed up some clothes and disappeared into the bathroom.

He yawned and stretched again. Those painkillers were doing a fantastic job, or else he was much more relaxed than he'd been earlier this morning. He snuffled to himself as he slowly rotated his arm. Definitely on the mend. If he was careful, he'd be able to talk her back into bed after breakfast. Didn't everyone need an afternoon nap? He certainly did.

Sophia emerged from the bathroom and headed for the kitchen. Rain took his turn and managed to pull on some clothes. If this was Wednesday, he had the rest of today to get back into shape before heading up island tomorrow morning to search for the van before it made the Thursday night run to return the workers to Cumberland. That should be enough recovery time.

When he entered the kitchen, he saw that Sophia had found bacon in the fridge and was laying strips of meat into the bottom of his fry pan. Perfect. He walked up quietly behind her, wrapped his arms around her waist and kissed her neck. She shuddered, and the effect on him was startling. Immediately, his body grew hard and he pulled her back against him just to feel the shape of her again. Thank heaven for afternoon naps.

"I'll make the toast," he said, turning to the counter. "I don't want to distract you from your cooking."

"All right," she murmured. "Don't make it too dark, and go easy on the butter."

"Okay." So she was picky about her toast. He was picky about his bacon. "I like the bacon well cooked," he offered, "no white fatty bits."

She snickered. "How do you like your eggs? Sunnyside up or fried to a crisp?"

He swatted her bottom with a hand towel. "Don't get snarky with me. Oh, sorry, did that hurt? Let me kiss it better."

As he bent to press his lips to her butt, she stared at him over her shoulder. "Rain? What are you doing?"

"Sorry." He stood upright. "Just being silly." He settled his mouth over hers and watched her eyes slowly close. Yeah, that's how he felt too. Totally enthralled with the sensations she elicited from his body. He loved her. It had come to him while they were making love, but he was certain. He loved her. Had he ever felt this way before? He wasn't sure, but he was sure about this.

She hadn't said how she felt. Perhaps it would require more time, and more seduction. If only his body would cooperate. This wasn't the best condition to be in when trying to seduce a woman.

Just then his personal cell phone rang and the cloud of smoke from the frying bacon triggered the smoke alarm.

***

CHAPTER FORTY-FIVE

Rain grabbed his phone and opened all the windows. Sophia removed the fry pan from the heat and turned off the stove as they made their way out of the apartment. Bertha appeared in the back yard, as did Ed from the lower suite. Apparently the university students weren't home, or were too tired to come down the stairs in response to the alarm, and the navy guy was at sea.

Soon the siren stopped. Rain had missed the call on his phone but saw it was from his folks on the farm. First he called emergency services to report there was no fire, just breakfast cooking.

Once they returned to the apartment, he cut the bread for toast, popped the first slices into the toaster and returned the phone call as Sophia pulled the pan of bacon back onto the burner with the flame turned low. To his surprise, it was Dad who answered. Mum was the one who did most of the communication with their children. Dad was usually out on the farm doing some task or other and unwilling to spend time on the phone. They only had a landline. There was no wireless coverage where they were located.

"Dad, good to hear your voice."

"Hi Rain, how are things going with you?"

"With me? Pretty good. I'm in the process of wrapping up my last case with the cops. Then I'll be a free man, or so they tell me."

"Free, eh? Well, that'll be a relief, I'm sure. We've heard from Jake that he's been out to see you."

"Yeah, he came a few weeks ago, or was it last week?" Rain glanced at his calendar on the wall which showed last month. A lot had happened in the last few days, he'd more or less lost track of time. "He's getting his PI licence in the next months, right?"

"That's right." Dad's voice sounded as strong as ever.

"How are you feeling after the heart thing? You sound good."

"Oh, I'm fine. The doctor fusses too much."

"Well, probably not. Heart attacks are serious business, you know, even if you don't want to admit it."

There was a short pause. "I know. And Mum doesn't need to worry overmuch about it, it's hard on her."

Rain pulled toast onto a plate and added more slices to the toaster. He put the phone between his shoulder and ear as he began to butter. "She'll be worried as long as the doctor tells her you won't take the medications he prescribes, or you don't cooperate with the tests he wants to schedule."

Dad sighed. "You been talking to Jake?"

Rain snorted. "Why, did he say the same thing? Might be time to listen up, right?"

"Yeah, yeah. I didn't call you to talk about that. We're going to be out your way in a couple of weeks. Toby Bonnar gets back from his travels, and we're driving out for a visit."

"Great. That's good news. Tell Mum to email me the dates." Dad didn't do email, or any other 'electronic gadget'. The toaster popped and Rain grabbed the next slices. "I should be finished probation in a few weeks, I figure. You know Jake and I will be out at the farm for harvest, eh? The doc said no more farming for you, but we'll come and take care of things."

"Yeah, I heard. Toby junior will be here too, he always is."

"Okay, that works. Gotta go, breakfast is ready." He snatched a piece of bacon as he watched Sophia breaking eggs into the fry pan, then dodged as she tried to slap his hand.

"You're just having breakfast now?" Dad's voice sounded disbelieving. "What time is it there?"

"Breakfast time, it's called a day off. Give my love to Mum." Rain put the phone down.

Sophia turned to him. "How do you want your eggs done?"

Rain looked into her beautiful face and saw the uncertainty there. He kissed the corner of her mouth, where the dimple showed. "How do you have yours?"

She smiled. "I like them sunny side up. I cut my toast in strips and I can dip the toast into the yolk."

He nodded. "I like mine that way, too."

***

CHAPTER FORTY-SIX

Rain checked his laptop. There was one email from a wrecking yard along the Island Highway south of Nanaimo. The owner had bought a truck the day before that matched the description he'd sent out. As Sophia relaxed on the sofa, reading a book, Rain grabbed his phone and called the owner of the place.

"Thanks for getting back to me, Buster. Can you describe the truck?"

"Sure, sure. Let me just walk out to the yard. The truck isn't a total write-off, although the owner didn't seem to realize that. He just wanted to unload it. But he drove it here, he didn't arrive on a trailer or anything. So, the vehicle will definitely be saleable soon. Needs a new front end, both the body and the mechanical. I think the right front wheel has been knocked out of alignment. Haven't had time to take a closer look."

"That sounds about right." Rain thought a minute. "How long will you be there today?"

"Not long, it's Wednesday, and the wife has made a deal with me, if I…"

"Yeah, I get it. I'm going to try to send a cop out to take a look, but if they don't get there in time, tomorrow will work. You there by eight, eight-thirty in the morning?"

"Yup. Somewhere in there. Listen Rain, I don't want any trouble. I paid for this vehicle fair and square, and I've got a receipt to prove it."

"Buster, don't worry. It's not you who might be in trouble. It'll be the driver of the vehicle, if this is the one I'm looking for, okay? No problems from my end."

"All right, then." The fellow rang off.

Rain called Morse in the Nanaimo office, but he wasn't on duty. Next he called Ross Cullen in Victoria, but he was out of the office, too. *Damn. Now what?* If this was Anton Ganaye's truck, and Rain could show proof it was the one that rear-ended him, he wanted to have the man picked up before the guy managed to just disappear.

He called Nanaimo again. "This is Dexter Winston. Is Vickers in today?"

"Hi Dexter." It was Marlyse on the front desk. Rain grinned. Some luck, at last. "Yes, he's in, I'll just let him know you're on the line."

Vickers answered with a disgruntled greeting.

"Detective Vickers," Rain said, wandering into the kitchen in an attempt to keep the call somewhat private. "I need your help. As you may know, I was rear-ended the other night and landed in the hospital."

"I heard," Vickers growled. "Sorry to hear that. But I don't know what I can do about it."

"I do," Rain replied. "I've been checking on a fellow named Anton Ganaye, and have since learned that a truck matching the description of his vehicle is in a wrecker's yard with front end damage that is a match for the accident I was in. It was turned in there right after the rear-ender, according to the owner of the yard. You know the colour of the car I was driving, you've got the wreck in the cop compound there. Now if you could send someone out to check this truck, look at the damage and the paint scrapings on it, you can probably match it up with enough proof to pick up Ganaye and charge him with whatever you can come up with in relation to the car crash."

Vickers grunted and there was a moment of silence as he heard a pen scratching on paper. "Give me the address," Vickers growled. Rain gave him the owner's name and the address of the scrap yard. "He'll be there for another half hour. You'd get the credit for wrapping up this case if you find the evidence." He figured any encouragement made sense when dealing with Vickers.

"I'll see what I can do," Vickers replied, his accent much less noticeable, and abruptly hung up.

"Let me know what you find," Rain said to the dead line.

He returned to his desk and quickly sent off an email with the details and photo Buster had sent him, addressed to Vickers, with copies to Cullen and Morse. He laid out everything he knew, and asked for whatever information anyone came up with. There, if that didn't produce results, then he would give up expecting anything to get solved.

Back in the kitchen, he called the Nanaimo depot again and talked to Marlyse. He explained his interest in a grey Mercedes, reciting the numbers of the licence plate for her, and describing the dent in the front fender. Was it possible for someone to call by Ganaye's house in Comox? If the car wasn't there, they should have a look in Union Bay. The vehicle seemed to be connected to both Ganaye and a fellow named Aribadis.

Marlyse indicated she was heading out on road patrol in a few minutes and would keep an eye out. Rain walked back to the living room, satisfied things were starting to come together.

He looked over at Sophia, who had been sitting on the couch pretending to read for the last half hour. She glanced up at him. "Why are you looking at Anton?" she inquired. Aha, so she had heard his phone calls. "What does he have to do with your accident?"

A little alarm sounded in his head. This was the one question he didn't want to get into. The thought of her with another man turned his guts inside out. But if Ganaye was involved in the case he was working on, even more reason to walk past the topic. It looked more and more like the meth lab, the grey Mercedes, as well as the black pickup and the van were connected. And Anton Ganaye seemed to sit right in the middle of it all. Best to distract her, which suited him just fine.

"Have you been listening to my phone calls?" Rain demanded.

"Maybe," she said, smiling. "This apartment is so small, it's hard not to."

"Those are police conversations," he said, a fake stern expression on his face. "All totally confidential."

"Ha." She abandoned the pretense of reading and put her book down. "That's what they all say."

"Well, I wouldn't know about that." Rain stalked across the area rug toward her. "There have to be serious consequence in response to such an infringement."

"An infringement? I don't think so." Sophia looked bored. "An infringement would be if I hacked into your laptop and read all your emails. An infringement would be…"

"That's enough." Rain stopped in front of the sofa. He paused. "Could you hack into my laptop?" At the sight of her self-satisfied smirk, he leveled a threatening look at her. "Take off your clothes."

She gaped at him. "My clothes?"

"That's what I said. Are you suddenly hard of hearing?"

"No. Are you? Because the answer is 'no'."

"What? That answer is unacceptable. Let me think." Rain half turned to face the bedroom doorway, trying to suppress a smile. He loved teasing her, she always rose to the bait. "What about this? I will, if you will. I'm offering a bargain here."

"Oh, a bargain," she replied, uncoiling slowly from the sofa cushions, giving his blood pressure plenty of time to elevate at the sight of her blouse tightening across her breasts. "I suppose that's different. Not a demand but an agreement."

"That's right. Something we both agree to. Are you taking your clothes off yet? You aren't going to drag your feet, are you? I've already got my shirt unbuttoned halfway."

"So I see," she said, eyeing his chest, which warmed him even further. "However, I wouldn't say halfway...."

"No? I can remedy that." He undid another button as her hands rose to the back of her neck. "Need some help with that zipper?"

"I think I can..."

"I don't want you to strain yourself. One sore shoulder between the two of us is definitely enough." He turned her to grab the tab, slowly lowering the zipper down the back of her blouse. "That's better." He seized the hem, lifting it over her head as she raised her hands.

Wrapping his arms around her from behind, he cupped her breasts with both hands. "That's what I call cooperation. Oh, Sophia, I love the way you feel in my hands."

She leaned back against him as he kissed the side of her neck and along the little nobs at the top of her spine. "We need to get the rest of these clothes off," he muttered. "It's mighty warm in here." He urged her forward, walking through the open doorway to the side of his bed. "I can do this, don't bother yourself with all these buttons and snaps. Too complicated for a little girl to attempt."

He felt her body shake in his arms as she giggled. "Don't worry, Rain. I've handled more complicated tasks."

"I'm sure you have," he murmured, "but I don't want you to strain yourself. I'm the man, I'll do the straining."

"What are men for, after all?" she whispered.

He snorted. "I heard that." Unsnapping her slacks, he pushed them down her legs. "Oh, sweetheart. You're so beautiful. I knew we'd need a nap today."

She turned to look up at him, a mischievous expression on her face, as he pressed her body down on the bed. "Is that what we're doing? Are we going to have a nap?"

Rain ripped his shirt off and heaved it on the floor, then tackled the button on his jeans. "Eventually. But we have some very important business to take care of first."

***

CHAPTER FORTY-SEVEN

Later that afternoon, Rain staggered from the bed in search of pain pills. He should have known he wasn't in good shape for two rounds in the sack. He glanced back at Sophia's golden hair spread across the pillow and thought of how she'd welcomed him so eagerly. He didn't regret it for a minute. That's the reason they invented painkillers.

Shrugging on his jeans and a golf shirt, he booted up his laptop. He had to wind this case up, he needed to get a life. Okay, there'd been a change in circumstance. The tracker on the grey Mercedes showed the car was moving. No longer parked in Comox, it was now heading toward Union Bay. He'd better get on this right away.

Seizing his cop phone, he called the Nanaimo RCMP office. When he asked for Marlyse, they patched him through to her car phone, but he had to leave a message. Things must be fairly active up island among the criminal element this afternoon.

However, it didn't take her long to call him back. She and her partner had received his message, and travelled to

Union Bay. They located the car in the harbour parking lot in time to see a big guy get out. He walked to the boat dock, carrying a heavy backpack, and climbed into a float plane. They could see a second man already seated in the plane's cabin. A dock worker cast off the ties and the plane taxied out of the harbour. "Don't know yet where they're headed," she said. "But we're in the process of finding out."

"Sounds good," Rain replied. "Let me know when you do."

He sat motionless for a moment. The financial information he'd searched out on Anton and his partner, Leon, had amounted to very little. Other than vehicles— the trucks, the car, and the plane— he didn't find anything of interest, no bank accounts, safety deposit boxes, nothing. How did they support themselves? Where did they work and where did they keep their money?

Right away, Marlyse called him back. "We found the flight plan, Dexter."

Rain always had to shake his head when he heard his undercover name. He still wasn't used to it. "Okay, where are they headed?"

"Going to Vancouver. I took pictures of the driver of the car. I'll send them to you. You should be able to tell who it is if you know this guy."

"Great. Thanks a lot, that's a big help." Within seconds his phone pinged—the photos had arrived. He didn't know Ganaye well. From his driver's license photo, Rain would guess this was the man. But Sophia would know better. Should he ask her?

Just then she appeared in the bedroom doorway, dressed

in a kind of floaty cranberry-coloured dress that touched her body in all the right places. "Holy shit." His mouth watered. He felt like a fourteen-year-old, noticing girls for the first time. When was he going to grow up? He tried to pull his attention back to the matter at hand.

"Sophia, I have a question."

She sauntered over to where he sat at his tiny desk. "Like what?" Her smile was smug.

He could understand that. He felt a bit smug himself. He grabbed her hips and pulled her down onto his knee. "I've just been sent some photos from a cop out of Nanaimo. I need to know if you recognize the guy."

Her smile disappeared. "You mean Anton, don't you? Is he involved in something illegal?"

He shrugged, rubbing his hands up her arms in reassurance. "I don't know yet. We're still sorting things out. Can you have a look and tell me if it's him?"

"Okay." Her body stiffened in his grasp as he clicked on the photos. She was silent for a moment, taking in the images. Then she shifted on his lap.

"Yes, that's him. That's their plane. They keep it in Union Bay and always fly together. I can see the other man, it's probably Leon. But that's definitely Anton, I recognize the backpack too."

"Good. That's a big help." Rain tugged her head forward and gave her a kiss. "Thank you for the nap."

She giggled. "Some nap. How's your shoulder?"

Her breast was right at eye level and he leaned forward until his mouth connected to the nipple he located through the gauzy fabric. He gave a flick of his tongue, causing her to jump at the impact. "My shoulder is feeling better by the minute."

"Rain?"

"Yes, I know, you want another nap." He leaned back and smiled up at her. "I can manage it if you can." His smile disappeared at her troubled expression.

She braced her hands on his shoulders. "If Anton isn't a cop, why do you have people following him?"

Rain placed his finger on the frown line between her brows. "I don't know anything for sure, Sophia."

"That's what you said before. Tell me what you do know." Her mouth had taken on a stubborn pout.

He pressed a kiss to her lips. "I think I've found Anton's truck. It's in a junk yard that I've done business with before, along the highway south of Nanaimo. If it is his, the truck has damage to the right front fender that would indicate it was involved in the car crash I was in."

Her expression changed to one of horror. "Oh, no," she covered her mouth with one hand. "Rain, I'm so sorry."

He pulled her hand away from her mouth. "It's not your fault. You aren't responsible for what Ganaye does. Only he gets to answer for his actions."

"Yes, but he did it because I'm with you. This is my fault."

Rain watched her face, wondering how much to tell her. He

didn't have proof for most of what he suspected. Therefore, why make her more upset over things that may not turn out to be true?

He frowned. "Sophia, I'm not giving you up, not even if your old boyfriend rear-ends me. But if he does, I'll sic the cops on him. I'm not afraid of bullies and I won't be made a victim. Nor will I let you be the victim. However, I don't know how he would know you are with me, or even who I am. So, don't worry about it."

He glanced through the window at the lowering sun. "Do you want to go out for dinner, or shall we order in?"

Just as the pizza arrived, Rain's laptop pinged, another email had arrived. The black truck in the junk yard belonged to Anton Ganaye and exactly matched the marks on his cop car for the accident. Vickers had issued a warrant for Ganaye's arrest. Then Marlyse followed up with the information she'd contacted the Vancouver police, seeking the arrest of Ganaye who would have arrived that day in his float plane in Vancouver Harbour.

***

CHAPTER FORTY-EIGHT

Anton put the bulky backpack in the cargo bay of the plane, and slid into his seat, laying a small cloth bag between his feet.

Leon glanced over. "Why don't you put all your baggage in the cargo bay? That'll just get in the way during the flight."

Anton ignored him, pushing his key into the ignition alongside the one already there. Turning both keys, he waited for the engines to warm before starting them. He waved to the dock worker, who ducked his head to untie the floats. The backwash from the propellers pushed them away from the dock and across the water toward the open strait.

"Off to Vancouver," he said into his microphone.

Leon shrugged. "I hate this trip."

"I know you do." He pushed the throttle forward and the engines roared, then with a flick of the levers, the plane rose, the nose pointed skyward.

Leon leaned forward as if to get his attention, although he was talking into his mic. "The last time we made this trip, the buyer was armed."

"I saw that." Levelling out, the roar of the engines receded as they began their flight across the channel. Sailboats floated below them like balloons resting on the dark blue water.

"And he had two bodyguards. What was that about? Did he think we were going to rob him? He should get his priorities straight. His bodyguards were heavily armed as well. It drives me nuts."

"This is probably our last time taking product over, Leon. Calm down, why don't you?"

"I'm trying to," he replied.

"Okay. We have to decide where we're going to go after this and how we'll support ourselves when we get there."

"I'm finished." Leon shot him a glare. "I'm not doing this again. I'm just hanging in here to get the last payment from this batch of meth, and then I'm finished. You can pay me out for the plane, which will give me a good start in a new place."

"I see." Anton studied the water below them, feigning calm. As usual, when Leon fell into one of his fits of anger, the rage that washed up caused Anton's heart to beat hard and his sight to narrow. They had just crossed over Mayne Island, and now there was empty water below. He set the controls on autopilot and reached for the bag between his feet, struggling to keep his emotions hidden. Pulling out the pipe wrench, he swung it heavily at Leon's head, connecting just above the ear. His partner slumped in his seat, his body held upright by the seatbelt.

A gust of wind hit the plane and jolted it sideways. Leon fell against the door. Anton unclipped his seatbelt, and rifled Leon's pockets looking for his cell phone. Then he reached across to open the door, unsnap the seatbelt, and shove the body out. It bounced once on the footrail, then spiralled down and down until he saw the small splash as it hit the water far below. Done.

Anton put the wrench back in his bag and threw it out the open door. The door banged back and forth in the wind, a few drops of blood trickling down in a thin streak. There was a small pool of dark red slowly sinking into the fabric of the seat. Well, it didn't matter much. A cop car had followed him into Union Bay today. There was no pretending now. This last batch of meth would never make it to market in Vancouver.

Leon wasn't the only one who had to disappear. But just not yet.

Anton checked the headings on the dashboard and changed direction. The flight plan might say Vancouver, but his destination had become Seattle. All he needed to do now was land at the unmonitored boat docks he always used, tie up and sell the meth. Then he'd carry on with his original plan.

***

CHAPTER FORTY-NINE

Rain left early Thursday. He had the drive to Nanaimo ahead of him, and the search for the hidden site, but he also wanted to meet with Jason Michaels again. Now the young man was starting to heal and had time to think while in his hospital bed, perhaps he had more to say about where he worked and who he worked with.

Rain was on the mend and felt remarkably better than even yesterday. His shoulder was still sore, he rotated it as he drove. But that would improve. Somewhere inside him, things were calm and contented. Satisfied, too. He grinned. Just having Sophia in bed beside him was so rewarding. Even when they weren't making love, having her in his arms as she slept helped him relax. He wasn't sure where this relationship was going but he couldn't be happier about the route they were taking. He pulled into the hospital parking lot.

Jason Michaels had been put in a secure wing, with a guard at the entrance. *Whoa*, there must be more than a few people under security watch. Rain waited while the cop examined his Dexter Winston ID and then made a few phone calls. Luckily Ross Cullen was at his desk and okay'd his access to the witness.

Jason occupied the room at the end of the corridor. The building was newer than the one in Nanaimo— no faded paint on the walls, or worn tile floors here. The patient was sitting up working on his breakfast. His face was bright red, the skin peeling and flaking off him.

Rain knocked on the doorjamb. "Hi, Jason. I'm Dexter Winston. I visited you in the hospital when you were first brought into Nanaimo. Do you remember?"

Jason blinked at him a few times, then nodded his head hesitantly. "I think so. Are you police?"

Rain shook his head. "Not really. But I work with them. I explained that to you last time. I work with the cops in a private capacity. But the guard checked my ID and let me in, so you can relax."

"Okay." He put his mouth back on the straw and sucked strongly. "This stuff is so sticky, it's hard to get it into my mouth."

Rain looked into the cup. "What is it?"

"They give me a protein drink every morning. I've lost too much weight and they want me to gain some back."

"Yeah, I can see that." Jason's eyes seemed too big for his face, his cheek bones standing out like swords above a sharp-angled jaw. "Why don't you just eat more food?"

The young man looked at him with pity in his eyes, as if he couldn't believe he didn't understand. "I can't chew that well yet. The skin pulls tight and then rips off when I chew.

They don't want my face muscles exercised that way."

"Hmm." Rain examined the tray, where a container of mushy fruit nestled next to a pot of some kind of pudding. "This doesn't seem like a good idea. What about steak and potatoes put through a blender? You wouldn't have to chew much, other than to get your saliva around each mouthful, then you could swallow it. But you'd be getting real food. Would that work?"

His eyes lit up. "I think it would. I'd give my eyeteeth for steak and potatoes."

"Yeah, well, don't jump on it too fast. You might need those eyeteeth." Rain looked into the excited young face and felt himself caving. "I could do something like that for you. We could give it a try, right?" He put up a cautionary hand at Jason's delighted expression. "I'm warning you, I'm no cook. But we'll give it a whirl."

"Okay."

"Now, I have a few more questions, Jason. I thought maybe you might have been able to remember some details that you didn't tell me last time. I need to know everything you remember about the bus ride to work—things like how many minutes on the ride, what did the scenery look like outside the windows when you got close to the place where you worked, who the other workers are, everything."

Jason nodded slowly. "I have nightmares about it," he said. "Especially about the fire."

"Yeah, I would imagine." Rain pulled up a chair by the bed and took a seat. "This is important. Just say everything that comes to mind."

"Okay. The windows in the bus were covered. Not when we first left home, but about fifteen minutes into the ride. The same on the way back. The windows were covered when we got on the bus and the blinds lifted as we got close to Cumberland, so, I don't know much. But I do know when I sat in the third seat the blind was wavy, like it wasn't properly attached or something. I could see a few things we passed before we drove into the tunnel." Rain noticed the young man thought they were in a tunnel, and filed that away for further perusal.

"One thing I noticed a few times was a bright orange blob, like a big balloon hanging in a tree just as we were leaving the tunnel. Don't know what it was. And Jerry, the driver, always had to stop and get out just before we got there. We all figured he was opening a gate. Same thing when we left, we drove a little ways, then he stopped and did the gate thing, then drove through and sometimes he shut it again."

"Okay, that's good information, Jason. Thank you. What else do you remember?"

Jason talked for quite a while, until Rain glanced at his watch and stood. "You've been very helpful. I can't thank you enough. What's the prognosis on your healing?" At his confused expression, Rain said, "What do the doctors say? When do you get out of the hospital?"

"Oh, right." Jason shrugged. "They don't really say. They're concerned about infection, with all this skin missing, so they're waiting for it to grow back. And the nurses cover me with some kind of cream all day long, so I need to be here for that. Do you play chess? I was in the chess club at school."

Rain laughed. "Do I play chess? Of course, I do. And I could whip your ass any time. I'll be back, with steak and potatoes and a chess board, how's that?"

The young face shone, even though it was red and peeling. "That would be, like, great."

"Okay, I don't know when, but soon. Take care of yourself, get better." Rain left, feelings of defeat and sorrow warring in his head. If he'd solved this case earlier, that young man would be driving his first truck, hanging with his buddies and looking for a new job, instead of being stuck in here, isolated, lonely, and in pain.

Well, today was the day. With determination and hope rising in his chest, he left the hospital for the drive north. On the way, he'd call Morse with the names of the other workers' families Jason had given him. Morse could call them and check that their sons went to work last Sunday as scheduled.

***

CHAPTER FIFTY

Sophia put the dishes in the sink and leaned against the counter, watching through the apartment window as Rain backed out of his parking spot. He turned the corner of the building and disappeared out of sight toward the street. He'd been very apologetic about leaving so early this morning, but apparently had some activity planned with the police force up-island. She didn't ask what might be involved. Was it about Anton? She didn't know. It felt like being caught in a vice grip.

Anton was a big guy. He was armed and could be very aggressive. He had a trigger temper, and if he wasn't a cop, then she couldn't imagine what he did for a living. Whatever it was, it was not only illegal but dangerous. It had certainly been profitable. When she'd lived with him, there had been no shortage of money.

Was Rain going to be on his own in this 'operation' today? He wasn't police, didn't have the gear or the backup they had, so she hoped he wasn't putting himself in jeopardy. That was someone else's job. Just because Rainier was on probation and had to finish this 'case', didn't mean he had to take on a role he wasn't trained for.

She shivered, folding her arms tightly around her midriff. Being with Rain was like Christmas every day. Something she'd dreamed about growing up, but was so much better in real life. He was smart and he challenged her. He made her laugh. He made her feel loved. Early this morning, she'd woken to the feel of his hands running over her body, gently squeezing and smoothing her skin. All the while, kisses showered down her back and across her shoulders. When she'd moved, he rolled her over to lay his mouth over hers.

She groaned with remembered excitement and longing. If she wanted to be the aggressor, he was fine with that, too. As long as they had sex, it seemed he was fine, in spite of his injuries. Giggling, she ran her palms up and down her arms where goose bumps had appeared. She didn't know what the future held for them, but she'd enjoy this while she could.

Turning on the tap, she sprayed dish soap into the sink. She had the whole day to herself. Rain told her it would be late by the time he returned. There was some laundry to do for her work week. And she wanted to have a closer look at those big bookcases in the living room to see what he had stored there. So far, all she'd seen were thrillers and science fiction. Maybe she'd put a few of her own books on one of the shelves. What would his reaction be when he found a romance in among the hardcore murder mysteries?

~~~

Kofi Aribadis left the cave early. Gerra would ferry the workers back to Cumberland in the van at the end of the day, but he didn't have transportation any longer. Anton had seized his car, so now Kofi was on foot. That was okay, one less decision to make.

He hoofed it back to his basement apartment and walked down the step to unlock the door. Going through the doorway, he glanced around at the room. Then he began to gather his belongings together as he sorted what to take with him. There wasn't much in the way of clothes but they were the most bulky items. He carefully collected his family photos, enclosing them in a folder and then inside a plastic bag. He didn't want anything to happen to these most precious mementos of his wife and children.

He didn't know what would happen to him now. Would he be arrested? Would he be deported? That was what he feared the most. He'd been preparing to sponsor his family to come to this new land. But he'd always known that without a record of employment, he was never going to qualify. The trick had been how to get out of this tangle he'd become enmeshed in and find a new job, a new way forward. His other employer didn't really count. Yes, they sent his pay through Western Union in cash. Yes, they sent him instructions on what to look for, what information they were after. But they were in the United States. The work for the US government would not help him in his fight to stay in Canada.

However, he was out of time to sort it out. Now he didn't have to worry about when to take those decisions, or how to extract himself. The time had come.

Something thumped overhead and he realized his tenant was home. He must be working nights again. That wasn't good. The guy might spot him leaving with big bags of luggage. It would be like waving a flag at Anton, if he discovered Aribadis had left.

He could deal with this. He'd leave down the lane and phone for a taxi to pick him up on the next street over. He couldn't walk to the ferry terminal. It was too far. So, he'd get dropped at the bus station and go from there.

Approaching the chest of drawers by his bed, he tugged the piece of furniture away from the wall. Reaching behind, he fumbled to find the envelope taped to the back and pried it free, laying it on the bed.

Then he dropped to his knees and felt under the mattress. Beds were complicated in this country. There was a mattress laid over a mattress, balanced on a frame with a set of legs. Why so complex? Back home there would only be…

Well, no time to think about that now. There were two more envelopes attached with duct tape to the underside of the mattress. Anton had forbidden him to open a bank account. But he was used to working with a cash economy. He ripped the envelopes free and pulled them out.

In the top drawer of the dresser he found the cloth wrap he had devised to handle just such an occasion. Unfolding it, he laid it out on the bed. He ripped the envelopes open and piled the bank notes together. The money here was very different—all this colour and design, so unlike back home. He arranged stacks of bills in an even line on the wrap and carefully folded it over. Then he removed his shirt and bound the cloth about his waist, securing it in front. Luckily, he was built like most Ethiopians—long and lean. With his shirt back on but hanging loose, the wrap wasn't even noticeable. He picked up the rest of the bills and shoved them in his pocket. Those would be for his expenses as he travelled in the next few days.

He glanced at the clock on the wall. Lots of time. The last ferry out of Nanaimo was the least busy, which was good from his point of view. He was less likely to be noticed or run into someone who recognized him. He grabbed his pack and cautiously exited his apartment. He noted with relief that there was no one around. Walking down the side of the house to the alley, he hiked over to the next block, thumbing a call on his cell phone for a taxi.

Most of the taxis here were manned by foreigners. It was a comfortable connection.

***

CHAPTER FIFTY-ONE

Rain had reached the top of the Malahat Highway before he contacted John Morse by phone. After he gave him the names and details taken from Jason Michaels at the hospital, Morse said, "Good work, Dexter. We need that information right now. A dead body has just been found in the ditch on the road out of Cumberland. It's a young man, no ID."

Rain grunted as if he'd taken a body blow. "Not again," he replied. "Was he burned?"

"No, no burns. Different MO. Looks like he took a blow to the side of the head. He didn't die there. He was dumped there."

"So, is it one of the workers that we're looking for?"

"Don't know, but could be. Now we have some names, we can visit the families. Someone will recognize him."

"Well, shit." Rain pounded the steering wheel with the heel of his hand, then honked at a brown car that had pulled out to pass him, changed lanes again to get in front of his car and put on the brakes. *What the fuck? Why do that?* The driver was either demented and shouldn't be driving, or had taken it upon himself to personally control the speed of the vehicles around him.

"Of course," Morse continued on the phone, "none of these young men would be reported missing yet. They aren't expected home until late tonight."

"That's why we have to do this search right." Rain hit the gas and passed the vehicle that had just passed him. As he watched in the mirror, the brown car pulled out to follow him. Rain stayed in the passing lane, not about to give the driver a second chance to box him in. He had no patience today for this politically correct driving bullshit.

"We start at noon," Morse said.

"Don't worry, I'll be there. I want to see this finished."

Arriving in Union Bay, Rain took the single road that ran the length of the village. At the end of the lane he entered Heritage Row, where the last remaining historic structures of the village stood. The school was an old building that had been shut down some years earlier but still had a large gravelled parking area. This was where the men in the task force were gathering.

Rain pulled into the lot with three police cars trailing him. Trucks and vans filled the area. Leashed dogs waited anxiously for the action to begin. Between the barking, engine sounds and loud voices organizing the crowd, the noise was deafening. Rain climbed out of his car, a bundle of papers in hand, and approached the fellow with the loud-speaker.

"Do you know where I can find John Morse?"

The guy gave him a gimlet stare. "Who wants to know?"

"I do," Rain said, impatience lacing his voice with irritation.

"Okay, why didn't you say so?" The cop turned and pointed to a white Suburban in the centre of the mêlée. "Over there."

"Asshole," Rain muttered and headed across the gravel, to the sound of the guy's laughter.

The SUV dipped as he climbed in and Morse looked up from arranging equipment on a counter that ran the length of the vehicle inside. "Oh, there you are. Good. I can leave some of this gear for you to tend. What's that you've got?" He pointed to the sheaf of papers in Rain's hand.

Rain laid them down on the counter. "These are my notes on where the place might be located."

"Okay." Morse tugged on his lower lip. "Show me."

Rain laid them out. "There are five abandoned coal mines within a ten-mile radius of Union Bay. My guess is the tunnel or cave we're searching for won't be too close to any community. The activity would easily draw unwanted attention. Also, one of the things Jason Michaels remembered today is that it seemed the driver, Jerry, had to stop the van and get out to open a gate. Sometimes he would stop again to close it after driving through. Jason didn't actually see a gate, the workers speculated between themselves as to what was happening."

"I see." Morse looked more closely at the map, then pulled out one of his own. "Here's the plan. We have six crews.

Each has a pair of dogs with a dog handler. We're sending two north of here, two south and two east in the direction of Cumberland. We pause to reassess at five o'clock. By then, word will have spread that there's a search going on, but we don't have much of a choice. The workers will be heading home at about ten tonight. So, we need to give it our best shot before then."

"Good." Rain thought a minute. "Will there be a roadblock going into Cumberland tonight? That way we find the van, the workers and the driver, Jerry, if we haven't already located them. We should be able to get some information that way, surely."

Morse nodded. "If we don't have any luck before that, we'll put a roadblock in place. Let's face it, this operation must be shutting down. After everything that's happened, they can't expect to stay in business, so today is probably our last chance."

Rain shrugged and nodded. "Just because they're crooks, doesn't mean they're stupid."

Morse put back his head and laughed. "Yes, Dexter Winston slash Rainier Murdoch."

Heat climbed his neck. "Okay. I asked for that. I'll shut up now."

"Don't bother," the police officer quipped. "I need your input. Let's get this show on the road." He exited the Suburban, aiming across the lot for the guy with the loudspeaker.

***

CHAPTER FIFTY-TWO

Morse took control of the loudspeaker and quickly organized the men into teams, lead by the dogs and their handlers. The teams set out, two going north through the town and into the hills, two going east toward the island highway, the last ones heading south through the hills and forests. To the west were the boat docks and the ocean.

Rain sat in the SUV, keeping an eye on the location of the tracker still positioned in the workers' van. It didn't move, but the search teams also carried trackers which told him how close they were to their target. Not close at all, as it turned out.

He called Morse by three in the afternoon. "We aren't anywhere near the van, and time's a'wasting."

Morse heaved a sigh. Rain could hear dogs howling in the background. "We're going to regroup at five," Morse replied. "We can set out new parameters then."

"Probably too late. Once it's dark, we don't stand much hope of finding anything. So, we've only got a few productive hours left."

There was silence for a moment. "What do you suggest?"

"I think we should take a few searchers from both the north and south teams and form a new team. Then we take the east teams, add the new group and focus on the old mines. I've got a plan drawn out here to show you when you get back."

"I'll think about it," Morse replied and clicked off. However within a tense half hour, he was back in the parking lot, a number of other men arriving with him, along with one dog and his handler.

Rain was just taking a small handful of painkillers when Morse knocked and opened the door to the back of the SUV, wiping his brow with a handkerchief. "Okay, Dexter," he said impatiently. "Show me what you've got."

Rain smiled with relief. "Sure. Here it is." He pointed at a new map he'd drawn, highlighting the old mine shafts around Union Bay which seemed to be congregated in an area to the east. "I figure the further from the village the more likely. They'd draw less attention. And here we have a couple of logging roads, not public roads, with three old mines nearby. Why not start there?"

"Gotcha." Morse leaned over the drawing, studying the layout as sweat dripped off his chin. "Where's the tracker on the van reporting from?"

"Well, it's faded now. No recent signals. But the last recorded responses were near those roads, although they bobbed around, as you know. There was no definitive direction. Still—that's the general area."

"Yeah." Morse gave a decisive nod. "Let's try it. Like you say, we're running out of time. And the van we're looking for has to be underground. Otherwise we would have found it by now."

"I want to be there." Rain straightened from the counter. "I'm coming with you."

Morse shook his head. "You can't manage the terrain, it's rough out there."

"No, but this vehicle still runs, doesn't it? I'll follow the search from in here."

Morse pursed his lips, eyeing the bottle of pain pills on the counter. "I'll travel with you. the others can take one of the trucks."

Rain shrugged. "Okay, as long as I'm there."

Morse issued instructions to his men and climbed into the driver's seat of the Suburban. "Let's go. No time like the present." As they left the parking lot, a pickup truck loaded with men and dogs pulled in behind them.

Rain held his map, watching for the turn offs. They trundled along the local road as he surveyed the countryside, looking for sideroads. "That's the building that has the power hookup in Leon Shankland's name." He pointed at a dilapidated structure on the side of the road. "Doesn't look like it's being used for anything."

Morse slowed and gave it the once over. "We had a look at it, it's got a water hookup and someone is living in it."

"Oh, okay." They traveled a bit further before Rain said, "Hold it, Morse. I think this is one of the roads. Look." He pointed to the left where a narrow gravel track abutted the road. It wound off through dense forest. "I think it shows signs of having been used recently."

Morse slowed, scrutinizing the map, then turned into the track, the pickup following close behind. The gravel soon gave way to dirt, and a small cloud of dust rose under their wheels. Then they were met with a gate barring the road.

"This is it. I'm positive." Rain unbuckled his belt.

"We don't know this is it. Stay where you are," Morse growled. "I'll get the gate." He stopped, engaged the emergency brake and climbed out.

Another man joined him from the truck following. "What is it, Morse? Have we found the place?"

"Don't know. Most logging roads have gates to keep the public from using them."

"Yeah, I know," the man replied. "That's why it's so damned hard to figure this whole thing out."

***

CHAPTER FIFTY-THREE

Morse waved the other cop back to his truck. "When we stop, we'll have another look at the maps and make some decisions."

He climbed into the SUV and put it in gear. "We don't know this is it," he said, eyeing Rain guardedly. "But we can have a good look and see what we find."

Rain nodded, excitement warring with nerves in his gut. The sun was lower in the sky. They didn't have too many hours of daylight left. He just hoped the tracker dogs and their handlers knew what they were doing.

Morse drove slowly, Rain monitoring the responder in his hand, but there were no further signals.

With a sigh, he looked up the steep bank beside the dirt road. "Do they really log in these conditions? How would you get up there to cut the trees down?"

The cop shrugged. "Loggers are pretty agile. I've seen all kinds of serious accidents come out of the bush. Men and chainsaws, it's a lethal combination."

Rain stiffened in his seat. "Stop. Stop the car."

He was thrown forward in his seat, wrenching his body as Morse hit the brake. "What was that about?" The cop glared at him, his expression impatient.

"Up there, on the hill." Rain pointed. "What do you think that is?"

"What?" Morse leaned forward to peer through the windshield.

"That orange thing hanging from the tree. Just a minute." Rain fumbled for the book in his shirt pocket. He hoped like hell he'd written it down. "Jason Michaels said something else, which I forgot to mention. Here it is."

He flipped a page and ran his finger down the numbered items. "Right here. He said it was bright orange, like a balloon on one of the trees when they left the tunnel. Does that look like a balloon to you?"

There was a mad scramble as men jumped out of the truck behind them. Dogs whined and pulled on their leashes. Morse showed the map to pinpoint where they were—very near one of the mines Rain had isolated. Then he pointed out the orange blob hanging from a tree up the hill from the road.

"What we need is a thorough search of this area. The tracker on the van isn't functioning, but when it did, it seemed to be in this general vicinity. Dexter and I will go further down the road to see what we find and come back in a bit. I want men on the road to ensure no one escapes, and the rest of you to cover the bush on either side. But especially up this rock face. We might be very close."

As the searchers organized themselves and spread out, Morse motioned Rain back into the SUV. "Come on, we'll do a reconnoitre further down and return shortly. Never know what we might find."

By the time they came back, having discovered nothing of interest, Rain's head was throbbing. They parked near the truck and climbed out. Someone called to Morse. "We might have found something, but it petered out. There was a track leading off into the bush that looked used, but then it sort of disappeared."

"Yeah," Morse waved him on. "These roads get a surprising amount of use with off-road vehicles and dirt motorbikes. Don't get distracted."

"Right." The guy climbed back up the hill toward his fellow searchers. Rain groaned. If he was in any kind of shape, he'd follow the track they'd found. You never knew what clues you might find, as long as you kept looking.

Suddenly there was a shout from a man up top who was working closer to the orange balloon. "We can hear dogs," he called.

Rain had heard them too, but thought it was the tracker dogs. Those dogs were straining on their leashes, not barking but going in circles sniffing the ground. None of them seemed to have found any scent to follow.

"What the fuck?" Morse scowled and began to climb the bank. "What's going on? Why aren't your animals leading you toward the other dogs?"

"I don't know," one of the handlers said. "I've never seen this before..."

There was a grinding noise and he and his dog disappeared through a gap in the ground. Then another man dropped out of sight. The noise escalated from below, dogs barking and growling, sirens shrieking, lights flashing, shouts of warning.

The other men crept carefully toward the holes in the ground, peering down to see where their fellow searchers had gone.

Rain moved closer, as shouts sounded from the road below, barely audible above the din coming through the gaps in the ground.

***

CHAPTER FIFTY-FOUR

Rain slid down the hill in the direction of the road, wondering what was happening and if they'd find the men who'd disappeared. Would they have to rig ropes and pulleys to lift them out of the holes? When his boots hit the bottom, the impact jarred his shoulder which caused the ache to kick up again. But that wasn't going to stop him. They seemed to be close—to something. He just didn't know what.

There was some activity visible through the trees off to the left. Cops surrounded a small group emerging from a gap in the bank, arresting everyone who moved. It wasn't as many as first appeared. One man, a boy and a couple of dogs stood together before the wall of searchers. The man had the animals on leash as they yapped and growled. A police dog darted forward and bit one on the muzzle. Immediately both dogs dropped their heads and cowered before the unfamiliar canines.

When he was closer to the opening, Rain realized it was a gap leading into a cave. The sirens had finally stopped but the lights were still flashing inside the cavity. This had to be one of the mines he'd identified on the map. The space was huge, the floor flat and walls carved, the cavity leading straight into the mountain. Kind of like a tunnel, the way the young workers described it. The two men and one tracker hound that had disappeared had reappeared inside the cave and seemed to be in good shape, although one of the fellows was limping.

Cops swarmed down the hill, careful to avoid the holes in the ground, and entered the well-lit space. Rain followed more slowly, knowing he likely shouldn't be in there but unable to resist discovering what was inside.

There were a number of workstations set up in the main area, each consisting of a propane burner and what looked like a cooking pot. Steam rose from the pots and the stench was overwhelming. Rain hunched his shoulders and covered his nose and mouth with the tail of his shirt, not that it helped a whole lot. The air was saturated with acrid toxic fumes. How did the workers survive in here?

The van they'd been trailing was parked off to the side. Rain got down on one knee to feel under the back bumper. The tracker was still attached. He pried it free and pulled it out to examine it. The device looked like it had taken a serious blow, likely from a rock kicked up by the tires. No wonder it wasn't working.

Garbage was scattered everywhere—glass bottles, plastic bottles, tins and plastic wrappers lay in huge piles against the walls and in the corners. A set of shelves built against one wall was nearly invisible beneath the packages placed there. More bottles, cans and tins—these ones unopened—plus packaged food and dog food, were stacked deep, overflowing in piles on the dirt floor. A locked cupboard, which one of the officers opened with a crowbar, contained clear plastic bags full of crystals— crystal meth, Morse told him. Rain had never seen the substance before, and was shocked at the quantity of the drug. Thousands of dollars' worth of stuff was stored here. He gazed back at the pots, no longer steaming now that the propane had been turned off. Everything came down to those containers.

Just then a shout erupted from further inside the cave, and two more young men were escorted out. One wore blue striped pyjamas and looked about twelve years old, although he did sport a thin goatee. There must be a bunkhouse in there, where the workers slept. These two were likely the second shift. They both looked frightened out of their wits.

~~~~

Hours later, ensconced at the Nanaimo police station with the four men under arrest and the dogs in crates, Rain learned the man with the dogs was Gerra, or 'Jerry' who drove the van. The other three were workers, two of them brand new at their jobs, hired after the burn accident in the cave.

The entrance to the mine had been covered by a huge sheet of canvas cleverly painted to mimic the appearance of the surrounding forest, which is why they hadn't spotted it when they drove the road the first time. The track leading into the facility had been disguised with old dried branches and fir cones strewn across its surface. The camouflage was well done and quite effective. If the searchers hadn't fallen through the roof of the cave, they might never have found it.

Halfway through the windup at the police station, Vickers arrived for his shift. He noisily blustered around, demanding to know what Dexter Winston was doing in the case room while the officers discussed their findings. Morse threatened to phone their station boss and wake him up to get permission to include Winston. Vickers subsided at his desk, loudly muttering under his breath every time a new fact was disclosed.

It was late when Rain left for home, and word had already come through from Vancouver. The float plane never arrived at the Vancouver docks. Anton Ganaye was still at large.

***

CHAPTER FIFTY-FIVE

Anton waited impatiently in the parking lot of the Seattle boat dock, two backpacks placed on the ground at his feet. His buyers were very slow to show up. It made him antsy and suspicious, given they'd been very responsive in the past. With everything that was going on, he was already on edge, but to be left waiting for hours raised the hackles on the back of his neck.

Perhaps these contacts were no longer reliable. Perhaps they'd been co-opted by the police and were setting up a covert operation to capture him in the act of selling the drugs. Surreptitiously he shifted, surveying the area. Nothing to see but mostly older vehicles, parked in rows across the blacktop. Nothing obvious to note, but they wouldn't be obvious, would they? That wasn't how the police worked. Maybe it was time to back off and lay low for a while. Things had already fallen apart back in Canada. Didn't the cops work together these days—cross border cooperation?

Just then his cell phone vibrated with a shrill sound in his pocket. *What the fuck?* He pulled it out and checked the screen—the siren from the plant. Glancing around, he flicked it off, killing the sound. *Now what?* This meant they'd been breached back in Union Bay.

He dialed Aribadis's number and waited, but no one picked up. Then he tried Gerra, and after a few minutes a strange voice answered. He quickly clicked off and shut down his phone so it no longer sent a signal.

Well, shit. It was definitely time for Plan C. Leon was gone. Aribadis wasn't answering and someone else had Gerra's phone. All that was left was him and the float plane. He glanced around the parking lot and spied a small posse of men threading their way toward him through the cars and trucks. They were plain clothes, but he wasn't fooled.

Grabbing the backpacks, he hightailed it around the office building and down toward the docks. The float plane wasn't hard to pick out, being the only one tied up there, but it was at the other end of the network of floating wooden fingers. Breaking into a jog, he wobbled his way along the unsteady main dock. The wharf was an old installation, poorly maintained, and the decking was uncertain with spots of rot here and there.

When he glanced over his shoulder, no one followed. Maybe he'd been wrong, just antsy and nervous because of the siren. Then again, maybe not. He spotted a line of men rounding the corner of the office building toward the gates. The adrenaline spiked.

Anton broke into a run. Just as he reached the plane, he stepped on a weak board and his foot went through. He fell, the backpacks leaving his grip and tumbling across the planks toward the water. In spite of the pain in his foot, he lunged for the bags. Uselessly, as it turned out. He watched one disappear over the side with a loud splash.

He crawled awkwardly to his feet. Looking behind, he saw the men were gaining on him. *Who the hell were they?* Forget the pack in the water. Grabbing the second one, he bent to untie the plane, ripped the ropes free, and hobbled up into the cabin.

Fumbling for the two keys, he shoved one in each slot as the men broke into a run. He started the engines, locking both doors of the plane from the inside. His foot throbbed as he frantically measured his distance from the approaching men with his gaze. *He wasn't going to make it. They were too close, coming too fast.*

On the other hand, he was in a plane and they weren't. He flicked the lever, sending the props spinning, and the men immediately slowed their approach. The back wash shoved him away from the dock, and he motored toward open water as the men came to a defeated standstill, watching his progress.

Hands in your pockets, boys. You can't touch me now. Plan C was definitely looking better than Plan B.

Soon he was flying low over open water, heading north for the Canadian border. Borders over water were a boon to guys like him. There was less surveillance, both border agencies careful not to infringe on their neighbour's territory. His chart plotter told him when he was nearing Friday Harbour. Turning north, he continued on for a few more minutes, then unlocked his door and pulled out the cargo he'd stashed behind the seat.

What to take with him? He had several bags containing food, money, new passports, drugs. But there was a limit to what he'd be able to manage. Best to stick to the essentials. Survival was the plan now.

He set the instruments on auto with the plane heading west. There were no boats in sight in any direction. Using his good foot, he pushed the biggest package out. Then grabbing the other bags, he leapt through the open door, only pulling his parachute cord when he was well past any possible damage the propellers and floats would cause. Below he spotted the raft, which had inflated on impact with the water. He just had to land close enough to swim to it and get himself and his bags onboard.

The plane would continue to fly until the wind knocked it off course, or it ran out of fuel. Then it would dive into the water and disappear. Easy, peasy.

***

CHAPTER FIFTY-SIX

Sophia woke with her early alarm, not having slept well. Rainier didn't come home last night, nor did he phone. Yawning, she threw back the covers and reached for her bathrobe, shoving her arms into the sleeves. She didn't really need it for modesty, but it was slightly chilly in the apartment. She grabbed the remote and raised the blinds to a lovely sunny day.

When she emerged from the bathroom, she stopped suddenly in the living area. Rain was stretched out on the sofa, his head on a cushion, sound asleep. His black hair was tousselled, the bangs hanging over his forehead, disguising the stitches in the skin. His jacket was thrown on the floor by the coffee table, but he still wore his boots. As she leaned over him, a strange, acrid smell emanated from his clothes.

She drew back in alarm. What had he been involved in last night? And why hadn't he called her like he'd promised? She laid her hand on his chest, but he didn't stir. His clothes felt disturbingly damp, as if he'd just come in out of the rain.

She gave his shoulder a shake. "Rain." No response. Anxiously, she placed her fingers beneath his nose, but he was definitely breathing. Pausing to catch her breath and allow her heart to calm, she shook him again. "Rain, I'm going to put you to bed."

"Huh? What?" Bleary blue eyes stared up at her for a moment, then his lids slowly closed.

"No, don't fall asleep again. Listen to me. You have to get up." She grabbed his arm and hauled on it.

He opened his eyes again. "Thea Sophia?"

"Get up, Rain."

As he gathered himself, she pulled and he rose to his feet, staggering slightly. "Careful," he said low. "That's my good arm." He gave a rusty chuckle.

"Come with me." She pulled him into the bedroom, backed him up against the mattress and unbuckled his belt. "Don't sit down! Not yet." Unbuttoning his jeans, she yanked his clothes off him, then knelt to untie his boots. When she pushed, he flopped onto the bed. "Here, let me get your shirt." She whipped it off over his head, then the tee-shirt, revealing his heavily muscled chest.

"There, now you can lie down." He collapsed sideways as she lifted his legs onto the bed, pulling the blankets up. He was sleeping before she finished covering him.

She stood at the side of the bed, gazing down at an unconscious Rainier Murdoch. His face was unusually pale with deep circles gouged beneath his eyes. He twitched as he slept, his fingers doing some kind of dance on the sheet. What had happened yesterday? Something, because he didn't get home when expected. And he was obviously totally wiped. Did he drive home in this condition? She was angry and concerned at the same time— angry because he'd promised to phone, concerned because he had exhausted himself.

Rain was known to never give up. During high school and his hockey career, short as it was, his reputation for dogged determination and persistence followed him. He was obviously in no condition at this point to take on these investigations he was involved with. Gathering his reeking clothes into a bundle, she took them to the hamper in the bathroom.

Then she lowered the blinds again in the bedroom and got ready for work.

***

CHAPTER FIFTY-SEVEN

Rain woke in his dim bedroom. The blinds had been lowered, but the late afternoon sun peeked through the western window. He rolled over. Nope, no one else in bed with him, he was alone. Sighing, he raised his arm and laid it over his forehead. Ugh. There was that smell again, the cloying scent from the meth lab.

He was stark naked but didn't remember getting undressed, let alone crawling into bed. *How did that happen?* His last memory was of stumbling into the apartment and laying down on the sofa. He'd needed a shower before going to bed, but didn't have the energy. He'd known Sophia was there. His truck had been parked in the right spot, although slightly askew—a girl's parking job that had caused a chuckle to rise up his throat.

She must have put him to bed. Heat suffused his chest. Did she strip his clothes off, or did he? The thought of her undressing him caused a twitch in his dick and increased the heat in his chest. He peeked into the living area. It was empty, and the bathroom door was ajar. No sound. She must be at work. He hoped like hell she hadn't just moved out on him.

He stalked into the bathroom, turned on the shower and stepped under the spray. By the time the water warmed he was definitely awake. There was an unfamiliar bottle of shampoo that smelled distinctly feminine when he squirted it into his hand. It smelled like Sophia's hair. He smiled at the thought. Too girly for him. Oh, well, better than how he smelled now.

Towelling dry, he noticed his dirty clothes hanging out of the hamper. That's where the offensive odor was still coming from. Gathering everything into his arms he took it into the hallway and jammed it into the washer, throwing in a cup of soap. *Would he ever get rid of that scent?* What about the young men who had been working there in the cave, four days a week, twenty-four hours a day? Maybe it affected their lungs. It was certainly acrid, and pervasive. He was surprised the guard dogs were able to live in that cave.

He dug out a clean shirt and an old pair of jeans and checked the kitchen. Nothing. She hadn't left him a note. He picked up his cell phone and sent a text. *I'm finally awake. Are you at work?*

There was still no answer from her when he sat down at his computer. Lots of news coming in on the case. John Morse reported they were holding all the men under arrest. The three young workers had lawyered up, under the steadying hand of one of the fathers. Mr. Gerra was on his own and ready to talk. He wanted to give evidence in exchange for a reduction in his own sentence. They were just working out the details on that and had advised him to get a lawyer.

Rain nodded. That made sense. He'd done the same thing when he'd finally been arrested. Just then his phone dinged and he picked it up. *Yes, at work. Glad to hear you're okay. You looked pretty rough this morning. How are you feeling?*

The heat was back in his face. He couldn't imagine what he'd looked like, but rough was probably a kind word to describe it. He rubbed heavy fingers over the scruff on his jaw, and felt another jolt. He'd better get that shaved off before she came home—if she was coming home. *Want to go out for dinner tonight? I can pick you up.*

While he waited for her reply, he glanced back at the laptop screen. The last item in the inbox caught his attention. The crew of a British Columbia car ferry that ran between Victoria and Vancouver had spotted a body in the water off Mayne Island today. A helicopter had been sent to retrieve it and take it to the coroner's office. "No word yet on who it is, or even if it's related to this case." Morse's words.

***

CHAPTER FIFTY-EIGHT

Rain glanced around the dimly lit Spicy Oyster dining room as he forked the last bite of salmon into his mouth. The place was packed, the tables shoved close together as waiters hustled around them bringing food and drinks to the patrons. Quiet music played from the speakers positioned near the ceiling.

"I'll have to go back up to Cumberland in a day or two." He watched Sophia's face for clues to what she was thinking, but her expression was smooth and blank as she nodded at his statement.

"I'm sorry I didn't phone you last night," he said again. At least that comment triggered a reaction. He would swear he saw a sheen of tears in her eyes. He reached across the table, laying his hand on the white tablecloth, palm up. She gazed at it for what seemed a long time, and he was giving up hope before she placed her hand in his.

"If you could have seen what was happening, you'd understand," he continued, squeezing her fingers gently. "I hadn't forgotten about you, but I was in the middle of a raid on a cave we found in the forest and things were getting out of hand. By the time everything calmed down, it was way too late to phone."

She blinked. "A cave? In the forest? Why would the police raid a cave?"

"Because we had discovered a meth lab."

Colour rushed to her cheeks. "A meth lab? Who was doing that?"

He shrugged. "We don't know yet. But the case is almost done. Should find out in a few days." He was pretty sure who was behind it, but wanted to be certain before he told her.

She removed her hand from his, covering her mouth with her fingers as a look of horror swept across her face. "Was it Anton? Is that why you've been investigating him?"

"Honestly, I don't know yet, Sophia. You'll know as soon as I do."

"But you think it's him, don't you? Oh, my God. Pete died from meth. You know what I mean. He got into a fight while he was out of his mind from the drugs. The other men killed him. They were probably out of their minds as well but the police think they were the drug dealers."

"Sophia, don't. Please, sweetheart. Whatever Anton did, whatever he's involved in, it isn't your fault. And anyway, we don't know for sure who's involved. It'll be a few days."

She nodded and glanced down, twisting the napkin in her lap. He looked at her plate. There was still half a meal there—asparagus, broccoli, most of a pork chop. "Eat up," he said. "I'm a very tired man. I'm almost ready for bed again."

She glanced at him, a sudden gleam of humour showing. "Ha, you just got up, the way I remember it."

He grinned. "I haven't even caught up from last night. I'm definitely feeling deprived."

"Or depraved," she murmured.

He shrugged good-naturedly. "That too. Are you finished? Do you want to take that home with you? I could have it for breakfast."

"Okay."

"Now, dessert," he said, reaching for the small menu in the middle of the table. "What would you like?"

"Oh, nothing for me thanks." She placed her napkin beside the plate. "I've had enough for tonight."

"Okay." He waved at the waiter and gestured to Sophia's plate. "We'll take that with us. Just need the bill."

When the waiter left, he said her name and waited patiently for her to meet his gaze. Her pale blue eyes were like bottomless wells, he could get lost in them. "When I woke today I was afraid you might have moved out on me."

"You were?" She looked confused by his question.

"I didn't see you anywhere. You didn't leave a note, and I had a shot of alarm that you'd left. Have you really moved in with me, or are you just staying there till things calm down for you?"

She shrugged and glanced away. "I hadn't really thought about it. I was supposed to be staying at Dad's place, but…"

"I know. Anton found you."

She focussed on his face. "Yes, so you said I should come stay with you…"

"So you think it's temporary."

"Well…"

"Because I haven't suggested anything else."

"No, I just…" She fumbled to a halt.

The waiter returned with a small box of food and their dinner bill. Rain dug in his pocket, threw some cash on the bill, and waved him off.

He drained his beer and stood. "Let's go," he said, holding the back of her chair. She rose to her feet, a confused look on her face.

"I need to talk to you, but I'd rather go somewhere private to do it," he muttered, hoping to get answers to his questions. He grabbed the shawl from her chair and handed it to her.

"Okay." She headed for the door as he stepped aside to let her pass.

***

CHAPTER FIFTY-NINE

Rain drove like the bad guys were chasing them, and pulled abruptly into his spot behind the apartment. Sophia was already halfway out of her door before he got there. "You could go slow," he muttered, "give a guy an opportunity to be a gentleman."

"Are you a gentleman, Rain?" She gave him a guileless look.

He snorted. "When I have the chance."

Inside the apartment, he dropped his keys on the kitchen counter. They landed with a loud thud. "Now, we need to talk." He waved her into the living area toward the sofa.

"I don't feel like talking." She stalked past him, dropping her shawl on the couch and walking into the bedroom. He followed close on her heels. "What do you mean, you don't feel like talking? Women always want to talk about stuff like this."

"Give it up, Rain. Stuff like what? I don't know what your problem is, perhaps it's the effect of all that acid on your clothes yesterday." She grabbed her nightgown and turned around to head for the bathroom.

Rain stood in front of her, blocking the way. "Stuff like where is our relationship going? Are we committed to each other? Stuff like that."

She gazed up at him with a blank expression. "Of course women don't talk about that. Men don't make commitments. What's there to talk about?" She stepped around him and locked herself in the bathroom.

Rain stood, undecided. This wasn't going well. He didn't want to lose her over a misstep on his part. *What should he do?* He whipped his shirt and pants off, leaving his boxers, which already had a tent in them. He'd better disguise that. He crawled into bed and leaned against the headboard, trying for a casual look. The bathroom door opened and he tensed, then waited.

She didn't appear. *What was she doing?* There weren't many options, given the size of his apartment. She could always sit on the sofa and turn on the television, but he would hear that. Then she appeared, standing in the bedroom doorway, her clothes slung over her arm. There was still a light on in the living area and he saw the shadowy outline of her body through her nightie. The tent in his boxers grew and he shifted restlessly on the mattress.

"Rain?" she asked.

"Right here," he replied and threw back the covers on her side. "Come on in. We don't have to talk."

She muffled a laugh. "I didn't mean it that way."

"What did you mean?" He watched as she laid her clothing on the chair beside the bed and walked over to climb in. Gingerly she placed a knee on the sheet and lifted herself onto the mattress.

He pulled the covers up and over her. "Did you put me to bed this morning?" he asked. "I was sort of out of it. Don't remember a thing."

"Yes, I did. You were sleeping soundly. You shouldn't work so hard, especially when you haven't recovered from the car accident yet."

Something eased in his chest at the sound of her soft voice. Her concern soothed him. "Yeah, there just wasn't much choice. I had to be there to make sure we put this case to bed. I'll be off probation when it's done."

"Okay." She took a breath. "You were looking after yourself. You'll get yourself off probation once you've finished this job."

"Kind of. I was looking after *us*." He leaned over her and drew in a breath, taking in her scent. "I want us to be together. But I'm acting undercover on this case. It doesn't work well when I'm trying to pin down our relationship."

She gazed up at him, but didn't reply. So, he kissed her just to persuade her to trust him.

Then he was caught up in the kiss, her smooth lips under his. His hand tunneled through the covers to find her breast and closed around the lovely shape. Her nipple dug into his palm and he squeezed carefully, feeling her, wooing her. His mouth wandered across her cheek and down her throat, his tongue tasting her skin.

He was so excited, he forgot what they'd been talking about. Just being this close to Sophia wiped his brain of everything but his focus on her body, his need to be inside her. "Baby," he whispered, "let me in."

Her arms came around his shoulders in consent as he hovered over her. He tugged her nightie higher to give him access, and his shoulder screamed at him to relieve the pressure. He shifted to his other arm.

His neck creaked, and he buried his face against her shoulder to ease the pain. He'd forgotten he was injured. Just driving home, or sitting in a restaurant for dinner didn't trigger any of these reactions. But making love to Sophia was an exercise in determination.

He didn't care. They made painkillers for just this type of situation. Later, he'd get some. Later, he'd tend to that.

Right now, he felt great. He shoved his boxers down and pressed himself against her, in her, as the tension in his chest slowly eased.

"Oh, baby, you're magical. I love you." He moved his mouth to hers and began a slow seduction that took him out of himself, his lips on her lips, his hand on her breast as he pushed himself in and withdrew, and once again. Then he moved his fingers down to where they were joined, rubbing her tender nub until she rose up under him, gasping for breath.

The excitement was overwhelming, and he came with a long groan, his face pressed into the pillow beside her head.

***

CHAPTER SIXTY

Rain dozed, waking when he felt Sophia slide out from under his arm as she tried to leave the bed. He tightened his grip, pinning her in place. "Where are you going?"

"There's still a light on out there. And I don't think we locked the door when we got home."

"I'll take care of it." He rolled toward the side of the bed, groaning as his shoulder pinched. He staggered a bit as he got to his feet, then steadied and walked into the kitchen to snick the old lock shut. He hit the bathroom for pain pills, turned off lights, and headed back to bed where he switched on the lamp on his bedside table.

Sophia covered her eyes with her hand as he climbed in and collapsed against the headboard. He sighed and smoothed one hand over her silky hair, rubbing a strand between his fingers.

"You forgot the light," she said.

"No, I didn't. We need to talk and I want to be able to see you when we do."

One pale blue eye peeked at him from between her fingers. "Do we have to do it now?"

"Yes, we do. No more putting it off. Just because you don't like talking about emotions, doesn't mean I can't."

She laughed. "You're a guy, Rain. You hate talking about emotions."

He chuckled and pulled her against his side, sliding his hand down to feel her breast. "But I can do it if I have to. And there are compensations."

"Give me a break," she muttered, shoving his hand away. "What are you so all-fired anxious to talk about?"

"At last. Some cooperation. And you can stop hiding." He pulled her hand away to gaze into her face. "I love you, Sophia." His chest was tight, but he managed to get the words out past the obstruction.

She blinked. "You only say that when we have sex."

"Is that true?" Thoughtfully, he glanced at the old beams in the ceiling above his head. He should have known she was going to give him a hard time about this. "Well, we aren't having sex now, and I just said it."

"It doesn't count. We just had sex."

He snickered to himself. "And it was great. I want to do it again."

"See? That's what it's all about."

"You don't want to have sex?"

She giggled. "I didn't say that."

251

"Because you seemed to be enjoying yourself."

She swatted his shoulder.

"Ouch. That's my bad shoulder."

"I know. That's why I hit that one."

"You're a mean woman. I love you, Sophia."

She stilled, looking into his face.

"Do you believe me? Because I love you. I want to marry you."

She caught her breath but remained silent, her gaze pinned to his.

"Did you hear that? Will you marry me? I know this isn't the most romantic way to propose. I should get out of bed and go down on one knee, but I don't have a ring to present to you yet. There hasn't been time to look after that."

"Rain, stop it." Her voice wobbled. "Don't tease." A tear leaked from the corner of her eye.

He reared back. "You think I'm joking?" Placing a finger beneath her chin he raised her face to his. "I love you. I'm totally serious. Why would you think I'm not?"

"Because you never had time for me in the past. I know I was a pest, when we were growing up. But I really cared for you. And you didn't even notice."

"I couldn't, Sophia. I was just a kid. I had to escape the farm. Everything I did was aimed at my goal of getting out of there alive. I was afraid I'd be trapped in that endless cycle of planting the crops, harvesting, the near-poverty of our lives, the reliance on weather and wheat prices. I was desperate to leave. And what you felt for me was a schoolgirl crush. I thought you'd marry Jake, you two were pretty close."

She blinked as another tear tracked down her cheek.

He brushed it away with his thumb. "Don't cry, sweetheart. I don't mean to make you cry."

"Jake was in all my classes," she said. "He talked about you, that's why we were close. That and I love your mother as my own."

"I know, sweetheart. I'm so sorry about your mum."

"It was no schoolgirl crush," she said. "I loved you then, and I love you now."

He took a deep breath and hugged her against his chest. "Oh, baby. you better mean that. I'm not letting you change your mind." He leaned back to look into her eyes. "Please don't lose patience with me and this situation. The case is almost done. There are just a few more details to wind up and then I'll be free. We'll be free. Probation will be finished and we can make our own decisions. We can live our lives the way we want."

***

CHAPTER SIXTY-ONE

When Rain left the bed, Sophia was still sleeping. He'd worn her out with his attentions. Worn himself out too. He needed more painkillers. Then he sat down at his laptop. More emails from Morse. Mr. Gerra didn't have a bank account, it turned out, or a credit card, but when they searched his apartment they found a hoard of cash.

Kofi Aribadis, or Harry Badass, the other man who ran the lab according to the workers, had totally disappeared. His apartment had been searched as well. No cash there, a few personal items, some of them obviously from Ethiopia. The police issued an All Points Bulletin cross-country to pick him up.

The body in the water had been identified as a man named Leon Shankland. Rain sat up straight in his chair. That was the name Sophia had given as Anton Ganaye's partner. Now he'd been found dead, floating in Georgia Strait. Couldn't be coincidence.

He shot back an email to Morse. Shankland was Ganaye's business partner, and Ganaye was the man who rammed

Rain's car off the road. Had to be connected. Had they searched for Ganaye?

Yes, Morse replied, *we did, but no luck. How do you know they were business partners?* Rain's fingers shook as they hovered over the keyboard of his laptop. Was there a way to keep Sophia out of this investigation? All he could do was try. And one thing he did know, the plane was owned by both men. He could lead the police straight to Ganaye's house. Just not today.

He glanced toward his bedroom door and began to type.

~~~~

Aribadis boarded the last ferry, carrying a backpack and pulling a suitcase on wheels behind him. Most of the other passengers were wearing shorts and tee-shirts, those crazy flip flops on their feet. He didn't find summer here as warm as Canadians seemed to, and his long-sleeved jacket hid his money belt better anyway.

The car deck was about half-full, and the upstairs lounges were sparsely occupied. Many of the late-night travellers on the ferry spent the journey snoozing in their vehicles. He had travelled this ferry often, going over to visit the immigration shelter in Vancouver. It wasn't that he needed shelter, he just missed his fellow countrymen. He'd met a number of Ethiopians there, sharing stories, talking in Oromo or Arabic. It warmed his heart and boosted his spirits each time.

He found the bus on the bottom vehicle deck and paid his fare into downtown Vancouver, grateful he'd set aside some cash to carry in his pocket and not left it all in the body band. What would be more noticeable than a tall, thin, dark-skinned foreigner with a big wad of money pulled from a money belt? Having people look at him suspiciously was the last thing he needed. His nerves were already shot from all that had happened.

When the alarm went off at the plant, his heart had jumped in his chest. But it also spurred him into action. There was no time left, he had to move and move fast. He'd stopped in Nanaimo to buy himself a cheap phone. Then had the guy transfer all the numbers and information onto it. Once he got to Duke Point to board the ferry, he'd tossed his old phone in the water.

Salt water was deadly for electronics, and now no one could trace his whereabouts from his phone, but he still had his contact numbers and the precious photos his son sent from home. Kofi would send off texts to select contacts with his new number once he reached the other side of the water. He stowed his case in the bowels of the bus, but kept his backpack with him as he climbed the stairs to get something to eat.

***

CHAPTER SIXTY-TWO

Rain made a last trip to the Nanaimo police detachment to wind up the meth investigation. Detective Vickers had made an appointment to meet him there but was nowhere to be seen when he arrived. Probably didn't matter. He hadn't been very involved in the investigation right from the beginning.

Constable Marlyse was on the front counter and took him into the common room in the back where John Morse was working on a computer, files spread across his desk.

Morse rose from his chair. "Winston," he said. "Good to see you. We're almost done with this one."

"That's good news." Rain seated himself on the edge of the chair the other side of the desk. "What's left to do? Leon Shankland and his involvement in it? Anton Ganaye? What about Aribadis?"

Morse raised his brows. "That about sums it up. We're looking at charges against the workers, although they've been released on bail. Gerra is still in custody. He's about ready to talk."

"Okay." Rain waited. "What about Ganaye? I think he was the lead man in all this. How did Shankland die?"

Morse sorted through some papers and came up with an official looking report. "Looks like a blow to the head, then he was tossed into the water from a great height. The coroner says that's an educated guess. He could have received the blow to the head from the rocks in the water after he fell. But the imprint in the side of his skull looks an awful lot like a pipe wrench."

"Shit." Rain rubbed his forehead, where the stitches had left imprints in his skin. "So who did that to him?"

"We don't know. But we've discovered from the sales office that the plane was engineered to need two keys to start it up. The two owners were Shankland and Ganaye, so I have to assume Ganaye was in the plane when this happened. We've issued an APB on him."

"Right." Rain thought about that. Sophia had been smart to run for her life. This guy was a very dangerous man. "What about Aribadis?"

"Yeah, we've got an APB out on him as well. He's a landed immigrant, but distinctive looking, so it should be difficult for him to get very far without being caught."

"Tough," Rain remarked.

"Tough? What do you mean?" Morse leaned forward in his chair, his mouth tight.

"He's travelled all this way, presumably to make a better life for himself, and gotten caught up in this mess."

Morse rubbed his jaw. "Mess is right. He'll be deported the minute his conviction comes down. No second chances." He glanced at the mass of papers in front of him. "Are you ready for the search of Ganaye's house? I saved this foray for when you arrived."

Rain laughed at the twinkle in his eye. "I'm in," he said. "I'm not in great shape yet, still got a sore shoulder, but my forehead has improved."

He lifted his hair to show the scar on his head and Morse chuckled. "Looking more handsome every day." He rose to his feet. "Let's get on the road."

They headed north up the Island Highway to Comox. Rain had made this trip many times, but always alone. This time he rode with Morse in one car. Constable Marlyse was in the other vehicle with her partner.

When they arrived, the street was empty of vehicles. As they climbed out, he said to Marlyse, "What happened to the Mercedes?"

"Sold," she replied. "For cash to one of your wrecking yards."

"Who owned it by then?"

"Ganaye. It had just been transferred into his name when he dumped it."

By this time Ganaye's front door had been bashed open and they all trooped into the front room. It appeared to be a standard bungalow, three small bedrooms, one bathroom, with a living room and kitchen. A single-car garage was attached off the kitchen.

They quickly spread out and scanned the premises, finding very little of interest. A fat envelope of cash had fallen behind the bed in the master bedroom. In the bathroom, the top shelf of the tiny medicine cabinet contained items a woman would use. Rain looked but left it alone. He didn't want to give his position away, and there was nothing there that he couldn't replace for Sophia if she still wanted or needed it. Nor did he know for sure she hadn't been replaced by another woman.

In the living room, an area rug covered the centre of the floor between a sofa, an armchair and a large screen television. Rain watched and listened as the cops moved through the rooms. One of the bedrooms was almost empty, the second seemed to be used as an office, the third was Ganaye's room, his clothes in the closet. Probably Sophia's also, but he hadn't looked. He tried to get a grip on his simmering temper as he balanced on his heels, pretending to be watching the search.

The floor squeaked beneath his boots. Something odd here. He bent and flipped the carpet back. Two planks in the floor looked like they didn't fit with the others. He knelt and pulled his knife from his pocket, snapping the blade out. He pried the end of one of the boards. It came up easily. "Morse," he called. "Come have a look."

Boots tromped into the room and Rain looked up to find himself surrounded by cops. "I think there's something here." The second board lifted and he stacked it to the side. The cavity was stuffed full of fat manila envelopes. They were crammed in, one atop another. "Cash," said Morse.

"Gotta be," Marlyse muttered.

"Probably." Rain dug the first envelope out and tossed it toward the detective. He used his knife to slit the next one open. Bills slid out, mostly fifties and hundreds, but some smaller ones too. He glanced back into the cavity in the floor. "Holy shit. That's a lot of cash." He should know. He'd been the donkey years ago, the one who carried the cash and put it in the bank, when he was in business with Sanderson.

Marlyse laughed and threw a duffel bag onto the floor. "Fill it up, Dexter, we've got a counting machine back at the station." Her partner got on his knees to help, and Rain finally left them to it.

While they were busy with the money, he searched the main bedroom. Lots of women's clothing in the closet. Either Ganaye had found himself a new female, or he still had Sophia's stuff. He searched the night tables. It was obvious which was Ganaye's. It held a couple of dirty coffee cups and an empty glass. The other one contained some items of interest to Rain. There were a few books with book marks inserted, obviously half read. But he also found a photo of the Bonnar children in the drawer, must have been taken just before the mother died. Randy looked about two years old. Sophia would have been twelve. She'd been pretty even than. Holding his breath, he'd barely fumbled it into his pocket before Morse came in. "Find anything else?" he asked.

"Not yet, But I haven't looked in the garage. Did you give it a thorough search?"

"Well, judging from the look of what you found in the living room, probably not thorough enough. Let's have another go." Morse turned to lead the way.

Rain followed him through the kitchen and into the garage. He already knew what it looked like, having been by this house a few times looking for Anton. Nothing new here. Same tools on the walls, same work counters covered with junk. But a hydraulic lift had been installed in the floor. He took a stick and poked around in the hole. "Yeah, I tried that," said Morse. "Didn't find anything."

"No, but we should test all the floors. He might have had more than one place to stash the cash."

"Good one—stash the cash. But you're right." Morse stomped back into the house, followed by Rain, and began in the kitchen. Rain found a few envelopes stuffed behind the refrigerator and pulled them out. They didn't add much to what they'd already found.

However, in the bedroom/office, Marlyse noticed some loose floorboards. Once Rain pried them up, a new stash of envelopes appeared.

"Dexter Winston," Morse said, appreciation in his voice. "I'll work a case with you any time."

Marlyse smiled. "Me too. I've never been so rich."

Rain chuckled. "You aren't rich, just loaded down with evidence."

She pursed her lips. "True. Still, it's been fun." Her partner stepped between them in a protective stance. Rain recognized that action, it was something he might do if Sophia was getting too friendly with another man.

He glanced at Morse. "Is the case finished? Are we done?"

At the detective's nod, a feeling of weightlessness descended on him. Hope rose in his chest. He was finally free.

***

CHAPTER SIXTY-THREE

Aribadis stepped into the entry of the immigrant shelter in downtown Vancouver. Nothing had changed since his last visit. The dingy floor was filled with mattresses arranged in rows, chairs lining the far wall. There was a bank of lockers in the hall. He could smell the despair the minute he walked in. Why did these men stay here? There were many jobs to be had in their new country.

He understood the intimidation of walking out unprotected into a world that was strange to them. That's what it had been like for him. But there hadn't been another option.

The woman on the desk recognized him. "Oh, Mr. Harababis," she called. Somehow, she'd never been able to get his name right. "We haven't seen you here in a long time. Do you need to book a bed for the night?"

"No, thank you. I've come to meet up with my friends."

"They're all in the dining hall. If you hurry, tea is being served."

Kofi smiled and waved at her, turning to continue on

toward the eating area in the back. The noise rose in volume as he drew closer, the distinctive sounds of the Oromo and Arabic languages rising and falling. He walked through the doorway and the place fell silent.

It took a few moments before the talk resumed. He was surprised how many men were here, having tea. Coffee was the drink of preference in Ethiopia, and most of these men were from countries nestled in the Horn of Africa. His friend, Ahmed, waved him over and took another cup from the stack on the table, pouring from the communal pot of tasteless western tea.

"Kofi," he said low. "It is very good to see you again." The other men at the table turned away slightly and continued their conversation to give them privacy.

"Ahmed. I didn't know if you would still be here. Have you not found a job?"

"Yes." He smiled proudly. "I have already started work. I'm the dish washer in a restaurant one street over. But I haven't made enough money yet to move into my own place. How are you? You look pale."

Kofi winced. A whitie would never say something like that to him. They wouldn't even notice if he was upset or 'pale'. He put out his hand and Ahmed seized it with his own. "Is something wrong?"

"You could say," Kofi replied. "The police are after me right this minute. I don't know how to get out of the trap I am in. My appearance is too distinctive here. I won't be able to avoid being captured. Then I will be sent home and my family will be in poverty again. It is tearing out my heart."

"Yes. I wondered about the work you did, that you had many dollars so quickly. Is that part of the problem?"

Kofi looked down in embarrassment and withdrew his hand.

Ahmed pushed the cup toward him. "Drink your tea, all will be well in the end."

He took comfort from the old saying, although he despaired that it carried any weight in this new world. He took a swallow and put the warm cup back on the table. Looking around, he noticed all of the men were from an Arab background, darker skin, large dark eyes, long thin faces and beaked noses. He felt like he fit in here.

Ahmed leaned toward him and spoke in his ear. "I have a suggestion," he said. "We need to talk in private."

"You do?" Hope sprang to life in his chest, even as he attempted to hold it back. "What kind of suggestion?"

"Come with me." Ahmed finished his tea and rose. Aribadis followed suit, traipsing after his friend toward the rear door. Out in the alley, he pulled his jacket closer against the evening chill.

Ahmed leaned against the brick wall. "One of the men from here was killed two days ago."

"What? I didn't hear about that."

"No, it didn't reach the news, but then it wouldn't, would it? We are not important enough to make the news."

He looked down at his worn boots and waited.

"He'd gotten involved in a drug gang and started using

something called meth," Ahmed continued. "I don't know what it is, but now I don't want to know. It changed him dramatically, he got very confrontational, and they were about to kick him out of the shelter. But they didn't have to, because he never returned. He died on the streets."

"No, that is very bad." Kofi glanced fearfully at his friend. This man would likely not still be his friend if he found out how he had been earning his money. People died from this stuff and he'd been involved in the manufacture of it.

"Yes, it is very bad. He is not the only one who has been using it. This drug leaves a trail of sorrow."

There was a pause as Kofi held his breath, wondering where this conversation was going.

"The thing is," Ahmed said, "Something good may have come out of it. The man who died left his papers in his blankets and didn't return for them. I have them now, and have been wondering what benefit can come from them."

Kofi raised his head, hope blooming in his chest.

"Those papers describe a man of about your age, from the country of Eritrea, by the name of Aiby Estefanos. Do you think you could be that man?"

"What are you offering, Ahmed? I'm not sure I understand."

"Just this. They haven't identified the dead man, Kofi. You could be that man. His papers are here, and if the police are looking for you, they won't find you, especially if you travel across the border."

His breath left his lungs in a gust of wind. Was this a good idea? He wasn't sure. But it was a solution that would allow him to try to put his life back together in a different country than where he now lived.

A cloak of grief fell over his shoulders along with a layer of hope. He'd been involved in the production of that horrible drug this man had gotten involved with, something that ended his life in the new world he'd chosen. Now he had to turn his back on the new country that had welcomed him in.

He still had his contacts in the United States, and perhaps that was where he should go. He had an opportunity there that had just been taken away in this country. He would head for the border tomorrow.

Kofi Aribadis vowed from that moment, everything he did as Aiby Estefanos would be above board. This new world and his own family deserved nothing less.

***

CHAPTER SIXTY-FOUR

Today was the day for Rain's appearance in court. He straightened his jacket and looked down at his new suit. Even his shoes were new, black oxfords with trendy shoelaces. His shirt was pale blue and accented the colour of his eyes, Sophia said. She'd picked it out. And the tie was very formal, like something from a bespoke shop in London.

Nigel, his probation officer had signed him off as having successfully completed probation. Rain was pleased to have it on record that he'd finished without any further charges. Detective Ross Cullen had written a letter attesting to his cooperation and success in working several police investigations.

Surprisingly, now Rain was applying for a complete discharge. If he could get that, his criminal record would be erased. It wouldn't be there to trip him up, to stand in the way of working with his brother Jake on the cases they accepted in the proposed PI business. All sorts of things would become possible if he could get the discharge. It hadn't been his idea, he didn't really think it would happen, but Ross Cullen had put the option forward, and offered to appear at the hearing to support his application.

Rain was amazed. Cullen had worked for two years to put him behind bars. Now here he was supporting him to have his record erased. The world was on its ear. John Morse had stepped up as well and would be appearing on his behalf.

"We'd better go," Rain said, his voice hoarse as he glanced at Sophia. She looked fantastic as always. Her skirt was just tight enough to raise his temperature, and the cleavage of her blouse had him excited and worried at the same time. Court was a formal place. Was her blouse too low for this?

She moved against him and he grabbed her eagerly with both arms. "You'll do fine, Rain. I've never seen you nervous about anything, not your debating, or your hockey games."

"Yeah, but there's a lot at stake today."

She kissed him. "True, but you've got two detectives standing by your side to testify and guide you through. You couldn't be in better hands."

He tightened his hold. "Nor could you," he joked, gripping the curves of her bottom as he laid his mouth over hers. She giggled under the intimate pressure.

At the courthouse, Ross was pacing up and down in the corridor outside their courtroom. "There you are," he said. "I thought you'd chickened out."

Rain frowned, bristling. "I don't chicken out," he growled.

Ross grinned as if he knew what he'd triggered. "This is Chambers. The judge is currently in session, and we're third on the docket, so let's get in there before we're late." He held the door and Sophia entered, Rain close on her heels. Ross led the way down the aisle to a bench close to the front of the room. Rain hadn't been in a courtroom very often and looked around with interest.

The judge was behind his bench, wearing black robes. The woman seated below him was using a recorder and taking notes as well. The guard was just escorting someone out the back door. When he returned, he announced *Rainier Murdoch and the Crown*.

Rain looked up in surprise, but Ross showed him the paper that listed the cases. There is was—*Rainier Murdoch vs. the Queen*.

He barely had time to orient himself before Ross nudged him forward and they went through a gate into the arena before the high bench. Just then, John Morse appeared at the back door, following them down the steps.

"I'm Rainier Murdoch," Rain said.

"And what is the purpose of this hearing?" the judge asked.

Ross stepped forward. "Detective Ross Cullen, of the RCMP, Your Honour. Mr. Murdoch was convicted of several criminal offences and sentenced to probation only. He has now successfully completed his probation as shown by the document from his probation officer."

The judge looked at Rain. "Congratulations, Mr. Murdoch." Rain lowered his head in acknowledgement. He wasn't sure, but the judge didn't sound sarcastic.

"In addition," Ross continued, "we hereby make application for a complete discharge. I understand that such is not often sought or granted. But on his behalf, Mr. Murdoch was not convicted of a violent crime. He was running an online gambling site, without a licence. More or less a victimless offense, Your Honour. In addition, part of his probation conditions involved working with the police to solve money laundering crimes. He has been most useful to us."

Ross took a breath. "I can attest to his complete turn around in the past year, Your Honour. I am not the only witness here on his behalf. I rest my case."

Ross stepped back and John Morse took his place. "Detective John Morse here, Your Honour, of the Nanaimo RCMP detachment. I have worked with Mr Murdoch closely on his last project with the police. We were unable to make any progress on this case, and likely would not have cracked it without his invaluable assistance. As it is, all the issues have been solved and the case laid to rest. If ever he chooses to work with the police in the future, I will be first in line to encourage him."

There was a pause as the judge finished reading the documents before him and then eyed Rain standing before his bench. Rain wasn't sure what to do. Should he say something? He didn't have a clue what that would be. The cops had already said it all. Perhaps he should endorse what they said, that he was a different man. It felt awkward. He was rescued by the judge.

"This might be the first time in my career that the police are petitioning for a complete discharge. Who caught and arrested Mr Murdoch in the first place?"

Ross stepped forward. "I did, Your Honour, and it took me nearly two years. I thought I was looking for a dangerous man. But that didn't turn out to be the case. I'm the one who suggested this application, Your Honour, and I strongly support it."

"Well." The judge rubbed his lower lip. "You know him better than I do. I hereby grant a complete discharge to Mr. Rainier Murdoch." He slammed his gavel. "You're a lucky man, Mr. Murdoch. See you don't waste it."

"Yes, sir," he said. The guard waved them out through the gates and called the next case.

Rain staggered up the stairs to where Sophia waited on the bench and motioned her out. She slid toward him, taking his hand and getting to her feet.

"Let's go," Ross said, pointing toward the exit. "We can talk outside in the hall."

The door softly bumped shut behind them as they emerged into the bright lights in the hallway.

"Were you expecting that result?" Rain still couldn't believe it.

Ross grinned. "I thought it was worth a try. I have to admit, I've never done that before for someone I caught and prosecuted, so take it for what it's meant to be. I believe in you, Murdoch. I think you have a good future ahead of you. Don't blow it."

"Ha, as if I would." He shook Ross's hand with a firm grip. "This wouldn't have happened without you. Thank you. And you, Morse." He turned to the other man. "Thanks for taking the time to come all the way down here, and for giving evidence on my behalf. I'm still trying to process this."

Morse nodded and shook his hand. "What does it mean to you, Murdoch? I need to get used to calling you that. Better name than Winston, I have to say."

Rain winced. "That's for sure. It means I can go into business with my brother. He just got his Private Investigators licence."

"For British Columbia?" Ross asked. "I know you're from the Prairies."

"Yup, BC. He wants to open a business with me."

"Good on you. You'd be great at that. If you need a reference, give me a call." Morse nodded in agreement, and the two officers turned and walked away.

Excitement churned in his stomach. "Sophia, I'm free. Can you believe it? And you're my girl. My life has turned completely around. What could be better? We'll get a house of our own, with room for both of us. You can continue to work with the police, if you want, or find something else to do. I'll set up shop with Jake. We've got our whole lives ahead of us."

He hugged her against him. "I think I need a nap," he whispered.

"Not a chance," she laughed. "You promised to take me out to dinner."

***

CHAPTER SIXTY-FIVE

Jason Michaels sat in his hospital bed, the gown rumpled around his hips and blankets pulled up to preserve his modesty. His face looked better than when Rain first visited him. Most of the burned skin had peeled off, and new skin was replacing it. Some of his beard wouldn't return, but he still had eyebrows.

Jason reached to move his knight.

Rain studied the chess board for a minute. He recognized that move, and the boy had done it too soon. He could wipe him out at this point, but it would be kinder to give him a chance to recover. Jason was getting better at the game, this was their third encounter in the last few weeks. He moved one of his chess pieces in the other direction.

Jason tried to restrain his excitement as he saw an opportunity to take the lead with his next move. He pushed his queen forward with his finger just as Sophia banged the hospital room door open with her hip. The dishes in her hands emitted a wonderful aroma. The young man immediately lost all interest in the chess board. He'd fallen in love with Rain's woman the first time he laid eyes on her. The food didn't hurt either.

"Jason, I've brought creamed mashed potatoes and steak pureed with gravy. You won't want to miss this."

"Oh, Sophia," he whispered, his heart in his eyes. "Can I have some right now?"

"Good idea."

Rain gave her an ironic grin and moved the chess board aside to make room for the rolling hospital table. He pulled a plate out of the picnic basket at his feet and set it down, arranging a fork beside it. Sophia spooned creamy potatoes onto one side, creamy steak on the other. Jason literally drooled.

"Eat up," Sophia urged. "It's still warm. There's enough to put in the fridge so you can have it for lunch tomorrow as well."

"Oh, man." The new skin on his face turned bright red with excitement as he stabbed the fork into the potatoes with sweating fingers. He moaned as he put the morsel in his mouth and rolled it around with his tongue. The doctors had actually allowed him to start chewing hospital food, but it was no comparison to what Sophia made. He mentioned it every time they played chess.

Sophia looked at the chess board. "Who's winning today?"

Jason grinned around his mouthful. "I am, but it's only because he's letting me."

Rain laughed. "That's not quite true."

"Yes, it is. You could have wiped me out back there when I made a mistake. But you didn't."

"Well." He rubbed a hand through his hair. "I didn't want the game to be over that fast. And you were just about to take my queen."

The boy snickered. "Only because you left her wide open for me."

Sophia began to tease, drawing his attention to his food and Rain thought back to the emails he'd gotten that morning from John Morse. Kofi Aribadis hadn't been picked up on the APB. Morse thought that was odd, having expected him to be arrested quickly given his unusual name and appearance, but there had been no sightings of the man. Maybe he'd gone down to the States, he'd written.

Anton Ganaye had not been found either. Given that he'd passed himself off as a police officer, an all-out attempt had been made to arrest him, but no results. Not even any reported sightings. Very strange. On the other hand, parts of a plane had been found floating in the water just below the American border, west of San Juan Island. From the reports Morse had received, the plane parts all pointed to the same type of plane that Ganaye flew. Nothing else had been seen. No abandoned boat, floats, sightings, nothing. The man had disappeared.

Rain couldn't decide whether to give Sophia this latest news or not. He watched her soothe Jason's excitement, teasing him into calming down and eating his lunch. It was cute to see. The boy was so obviously infatuated, he had to laugh. But he could sympathize too. He was in the same position. Totally infatuated.

Luckily, she said she loved him in return. He believed her, because she'd agreed to marry him. The very idea got his heart pounding faster. Now that things had calmed down, he was going to make that happen as soon as possible.

***

EPILOGUE

In one of the upstairs bedrooms of the Murdoch family home miles outside of the city of Moose Jaw, Sophia climbed into bed and snuggled up beside Rain, who was already snoring. They had started harvesting the crop yesterday, the combine running dawn to dusk. Everyone was here. Sophia and Leah helped Mrs. Murdoch with all the cooking and baking for the crew. Mr. Murdoch and his two sons, plus her brothers Toby, Ted and Randy had all pitched in.

Dad, back from Thailand in time for her wedding the week before, had proudly walked her down the aisle of the local church to where Rain waited by the altar, a small smile on his handsome face, his black hair groomed within an inch of it's life. It had been so good to come home for the wedding. She'd forgotten how right it felt to attend church and promised Rain they'd find their own church when they went back to Victoria, which was home now.

Everyone in this small community knew the Bonnars and the Murdochs. All their neighbours had turned out for the ceremony, and then put on a wonderful dinner and dance in the community hall afterward. She hadn't done the two-step or the schottische in so long she'd almost forgotten how. But like Rain said, you don't forget your roots. She snuggled closer to his heat and even in sleep, he wrapped one arm around her, which promptly went limp as he dozed off again.

Her brother, Toby, was in charge of the harvest, directing the truck loads of wheat to the granaries at the railroad station once the home granary had been filled. The loads of chaff were destined for the silo he'd erected near the Murdoch barns. Toby was taking over the Murdoch farm. Come spring, he'd be the one planting the next crop. They'd all promised to come out to help. He was very excited, with big plans for the place. The silo of chaff was for the animals he hoped to raise—chickens, ducks, pigs.

She fingered her wedding ring under the covers, still not used to the feel of it on her hand. She was a married woman now. The thought was profoundly moving. To get married was a huge step for anyone to take, but to marry Rainier—something she'd dreamed about as a girl—was almost devastating in its impact.

How her life had changed since leaving Moose Jaw for the coast in the company of Anton Ganaye. He had fooled her into thinking he was someone other than himself. When she thought of it, she felt so foolish. But Rain always told her not to dwell on it. She wasn't the only one who'd been fooled by Anton. But she'd been smart enough to leave him in order to protect herself once she realized who he really was.

She yawned and rolled over. The alarm was set for early morning. The men would be prepared for another day of hard work, the women needed to have breakfast on the table before the crew headed out to fire up the equipment. And her husband always wanted to make love first thing in the morning.

Just then Rain rolled toward her. He pulled her into his embrace and wrapped one hand around hers. "Did I ever tell you the story about the Bonnar kids," he whispered in her ear. "It goes like this...." He settled her head on his broad shoulder.

"Once upon a time, there was a family of children called the Bonnars. There were six of them, two girls and four boys. Each one of them was strong, so strong that other kids walked carefully around them out of respect. They were known all over the country for how strong they were.

"Each one of them was smart, so smart that the other kids asked them questions all the time, checking to see if they'd gotten their own facts right. Everyone knew how clever they were. No one was smarter than the Bonnar children.

"Each one of them was kind. No one was kinder..."

Sophia felt tears well in her eyes. This was the story he'd told her younger siblings to soothe and comfort them after Mother died. As he droned on with his tale, she fell asleep to the soft sound of her husband's voice as he fabricated a story designed to heal her soul.

*****
****
***

Note to Reader -

I would really like your help. Book reviews are the lifeblood of what I do and your review of my book would mean a lot to me. If you would take a moment or two and leave your review wherever you purchased the book, that would be wonderful. I honestly thank you.

Last but not least, if you find an error in this book, please email me at sylviegraysonauthor@gmail.com . This will help me fix things that my editors and I might have overlooked and make for a better read for others. In return, by way of showing my gratitude, I will send you a free copy of the next book with my sincere thanks.

Sylvie Grayson

You can email me at sylviegraysonauthor@gmail.com

You can learn more from my website at -
www.sylviegrayson.com
Or follow me on BookBub **at**
https://www.bookbub.com/profile/sylvie-grayson
Follow me on Facebook at
https://www.facebook.com/sylvie.grayson

THE LIES HE TOLD ME, by Sylvie Grayson

When Chloe Bowman's husband disappears, never did she imagine that in the midst of the search to find him, she'd discover she didn't really know this man at all. She's left alone with her young son and a time bomb on her hands. Lurking in the shadows is the mysterious Rainman.

Police Detective Ross Cullen was already investigating Chloe's husband when he disappeared. But the deeper Ross digs the less he knows, and the more he's attracted to the young wife as she struggles to put her life back together. Can Ross break through the Rainman's disguises to solve the case so he can be with Chloe?

This is the first time that I read a book written by Sylvie Grayson. The Lies He Told Me is an enjoyable read with several charming characters! There's a lot of twists and turns in this story, and it's also filled with mystery, suspense, and intrigue; all this with a touch of romance!

It tells the story of Chloe, her son Davey, and Police Detective Ross Cullen. Chloe discovered she never knew the man, Jeff, who she had married . . . he simply vanished from her life! That's when Ross, who is investigating her husband's disappearance, enters her life and comes to her rescue. Will he be able to help her? Will he discover the true identity of Jeff? Together they embark on a journey of discovery, of lies, and secrets. But with spending lots of time close to Chloe, sparks will flare. However, Ross never intended to fall in love with her.

Jake never expected his investigations would prove deadly

DON'T MOVE

LIES HE TOLD, BOOK THREE

Don't Move, Lies He Told: Book Three

Tagline— Jake never expected his investigations would prove deadly.

Sylvie Grayson delivers another thrilling romantic mystery that will keep you on the edge of your seat— a gripping story of suspense with characters that you'll root for and a plot that pulls you in.

After years of taking courses and jumping through hoops to get licensed, Jake Murdoch is more than ready to open his private investigator's office. Leah Bonnar, a family friend and childhood irritant who blames him for a past disaster in her life, steps in to volunteer as his assistant. Given he's not making money yet, he needs her help to get things up and running. Yet as the cases start pouring in, she organizes the hell out of him. Jake is attracted to Leah, and grudgingly grateful for her help in equal measure. Despite their history, their relationship heats up.

But in the midst of one of his investigations, Jake steps on the toes of a couple of very determined con men and Leah is sitting right in the crosshairs of their revenge. Can Jake find the evidence he needs to stop the criminals, while protecting Leah from their efforts to bring his investigation to a halt?

DEAD WRONG, by Sylvie Grayson

When Shelley's boyfriend disappeared, never did she imagine he'd come back to haunt her.

Shelley Blake is a nine-year-old child prodigy in a sixth-grade classroom when she first meets Chris Wright. He's the big boy in the desk behind who takes her under his protective wing.

But soon she leaves him behind to attend a different school

and skip another grade. When she begins university, her classmates observe her extreme youth and walk a wide berth around her. Lonely, she meets charming Billy Zach, but new love soon turns sour. Then Billy disappears.

Years later, Chris appears again in Shelley's life and she wonders if she can trust her growing attraction to him. She's already dealing with her father's worsening emphysema, her sister's secrets, and the demands of her still fledgling business, When the police return, asking questions about Billy Zach, and more evidence is uncovered, Shelley realizes none of it will matter if she's heading to prison for a murder she didn't commit.

FALSE CONFESSION, by Sylvie Grayson

Did Glory fall for the wrong man, or is someone lying?

Music teacher Glory has given up on men, with good reason. Then she meets the handsome lead guitar player in the band she has just joined.

Alex, body builder and construction foreman, is determinedly single because he's given up on women. But that's before he meets the keyboard player who just joined his brother's rock band. Suddenly his interest is revived and he goes on a crusade to gain Glory's attention.

But when Alex disappears and the police claim they have a confession giving damning evidence against him, Glory must make a decision. Can she trust the man she's fallen for, or has she been fooled into believing a lie?

LEGAL OBSTRUCTION, by Sylvie Grayson

When Emily Drury takes a job as legal counsel for an import-export company, she does it because she needs to get away to safety.

Joe Tanner counts himself lucky. He's charmed a successful big city lawyer into heading up the legal department of his rapidly expanding business. But why would a beautiful woman who could easily make partner in a high profile law firm give it all up to come to Bonnie? As Joe realizes she has become essential to his happiness, his first reaction is to protect her. But he doesn't know the whole story.

Can Emily trust him enough to divulge her secret? And will he learn what he needs to know in time to stop the avalanche that's gaining speed as it races down the hill toward her?

I loved this book! I've found my new favorite author.

Emily is a fiercely professional woman who is on her own and determined to protect her little family. Joe is a solitary guy who often doesn't deal with problems until they are front and center. But boy does Emily wake him up and does he take notice. Add in a wildcard assistant and a few unsavory characters and I was up all night finishing the book to find out what happens.

MOON SHINE, by Sylvie Grayson

Some secrets are too dangerous to keep…

A thrilling novel of romantic suspense from author Sylvie Grayson.

After losing her husband to a deadly illness, Julia Butler is
determined to look after her family, but this is the 1930's and
times are tough for everyone. As the endless string of jobless
men trudges past her farm, she does her best to hang on.
Then two strangers suddenly appear at her home. They are

hiding something that places her family in danger, and nothing will ever be the same.

Dr. Will Stofford has become disillusioned with women. In an effort to heal his broken heart, he leaves his brothers behind and sets up his medical practice in the Kootenays where no one knows him.

Meeting Julia throws his plans into chaos. Will can't turn his back a challenge and he won't rest until he solves this puzzle and puts things right.

In the 1930's, can a country doctor and a determined widow save the lives of these abandoned strangers?

I really enjoyed this book! It's well written with charming characters like Julia Butler, her two children, Maggie and Jims, and Dr. Will Stofford.

MOON SHINE tells the story of Julia, a young widow with two young children living on a farm in rural Canada in the 1930's. It's set during the Depression when men had to wander the roads to find jobs to help their families. These times were rough. However, two surprise visitors are discovered hiding on her farm. Danger lurks around her. I really enjoyed this book. It is well written with a strong female main character and a beautiful storyline with hardship and pain as well as love. I found it hard to put down and read it in one sitting. Looking forward to reading more of her work.

MY BEST MISTAKE, by Sylvie Grayson

Sometimes you get a second chance.

Jordie was heartbroken when he returned to town to find
Jenny had married another man. Now she lives beside him,
and he'll either go crazy or do what he should have done
before - claim her for his own. Jenny is back and she's angry,
her husband cheated and she can't let it go. But when her

boss dies and someone comes after her, who will she turn to? Can Jordie help put her life back together?

Jenny has already made a big mistake. Can she risk her heart again, or will this just be another one?

I found this a very intriguing story -- Jenny is a multi-layered clever woman who is trying to put her life back together after a bad divorce. Yes, she's made some mistakes, but as things progress, she's determined not to make the same ones again. She's afraid that Jordie might be one of those mistakes. Her job is to patch her life back together. Well written with lots of action and great characters. I'm looking for Grayson's next book.

SUSPENDED ANIMATION, by Sylvie Grayson

Be careful who you trust...

Katy Dalton worked hard to save her money. And letting her friend Bruno invest it seemed like a safe bet. But her job disappears and she needs her money back, everything Bruno has already loaned to Rome Trucking. When Katy insists he return her money, Bruno stops answering his phone and bad things start to happen.

Brett Rome is frustrated. The last thing he wants to do is leave a promising career in hockey to come home and run his ailing father's trucking company. What he discovers is not the successful business that he remembers, but one that is teetering on the very edge of bankruptcy and a young woman demanding the return of the money she invested.

With the company in chaos, Brett hires her. But danger lurks in the form of Bruno's dubious associates. What secret are they hiding and why are they willing to kill Katy? Can Brett put this broken picture back together, and is Katy part of the solution or the problem?

A thrilling roller coaster of a story... Interesting characters, family conflicts and divided loyalties make this a book that kept me up half the night. Brett Rome is a hockey player with a bright future called home when his father has a heart attack. Worse, the company is in serious financial trouble. Katy Dalton reminds me of Shelley Long on Cheers although she's brunette, not blonde. She arrives at Rome Trucking searching for money she's 'invested' through a friend
Sylvie Grayson has found her niche, you'll love this book...

Sci-fi/ fantasy from Sylvie Grayson

KHANDARKEN RISING, THE LAST WAR: BOOK
ONE, by Sylvie Grayson

The Emperor has been defeated. New countries have arisen
from the ashes of the old Empire. The citizens swear they will
never need to fight again after that long and painful war.

Bethlehem Farmer is helping her brother Abram run
Farmer Holdings in south Khandarken after their father died
in the final battles. She is looking after the dispossessed,

keeping the farm productive and the talc mine working in the hills behind their land. But when Abram takes a trip with Uncle Jade into the northern territory and disappears without a trace, she's left on her own. Suddenly things are not what they seem and no one can be trusted.

Major Dante Regiment is sent by his father, the General of Khandarken, to find out what the situation is at Farmer Holdings. What he sees shakes him to the core and fuels his grim determination to protect Bethlehem at all cost, even with his life.

Ms Grayson has created a fascinating new world with a lot of the same old problems. Sci fi and fantasy rolled into one with a sure hand and enormous imagination

I couldn't help but think a feeling of deja vu. Like I had heard this story before or like it reminded me of something. And then it hit me. It sounded similar to the fall of the Ottoman Empire after WW1. The new countries that came forth. The battles. The new rulers and emperors fighting to keep their territory. And the citizens, adjusting to the new normal.

And then I realized that this story is one of a kind. It has so many unique characteristics- personal relationships are intriguing, names are cool, the plot gets thicker with each page, and I loved the author's style. It became evident that I was addicted to reading the book. I'm going to give this a strong recommendation. It's my kind of book.

SON OF THE EMPEROR, THE LAST WAR: BOOK TWO, by Sylvie Grayson

From the mud and danger of the open road to the welcoming arms of the Sanctuary, from attacks by the dispossessed army to the storms of the open sea, Son of the Emperor takes us on a wild ride into danger and on to the dream of freedom.

The Emperor is defeated yet already unrest is growing in the north of Khandarken. After Julianne Adjudicator's father disappears, she seeks to escape the clutches of her vicious stepmother Zanata, and flees to the Sanctuary. This is the safest place for a woman in a hostile world of unrest and roving dispossessed. But when Julianne seeks asylum, it soon becomes clear all is not as it first appeared.

Then Abe Farmer arrives at the Sanctuary seeking medical help. Abe isn't interested in taking a young woman with them, as he and his injured bodyguard struggle to return to the Southern Territory. Yet when he discovers her fate if she stays, he finds he has no choice.

But the journey becomes more dangerous as they encounter the army of the New Emperor and are caught in the middle of a firefight as they flee toward the Catastrophic Ocean. Can Abe keep her safe till they reach home?

...a whole new world with the same old problems - fantasy at its best...

Really a powerful portrayal of how a society deals with massive upheaval - and at the same time a great adventure filled with action, thrills and even romance. Sylvie Grayson really knows how to tell a powerful tale. Strong plot, string characters that readers get invested in. Amazingly strong world-building. What more could one ask for? Enjoy.

TRUTH AND TREACHERY, THE LAST WAR: BOOK THREE, by Sylvie Grayson

When Emperor Carlton makes an offer to Cownden Lanser, can he refuse? Lanser has his own ambitions and Carlton may be offering everything he's dreamed of.

The Young Emperor has been backed into a corner. He holds a bit of land in Legitamia where he marshals his troops, but the skirmishes they've launched to expand his empire have had limited success. Now, his ambitions are aimed at overthrowing everything Khandarken has cobbled together since the Last War.

Cownden Lanser, Chief Constable of Khandarken, is a private man with a close connection to the Old Empire that he doesn't divulge to anyone. Although he's dedicated to his position, things are not what they seem in the rank and file of the police.

Selanna Nettles is a sookie, trained in Legitamia but working near her family in the Western Territory, healing the mine workers. But her life takes a startling turn when Chief Cownden Lanser hires her to attend a set of high-level meetings.

When these three meet up in Legitamia, the result is explosive. Not just for them but for the future of Khandarken. The Emperor makes Cownden an offer that might be everything he's secretly dreamed of. How can he refuse?

The Last War series is a stunning portrayal of a new world created from fire and consumed at the edges... sci fi/fantasy at its best...
Ok, this series is just getting better and better. The increasing complexity of the characters and the development of lead characters is a pleasure to read. The plot, with its twists and turns, intrigue and adventure, is a real joy. If you liked the first two books in The Last War series (and, seriously, that's the place to start before reading this book - it's worth doing) then you will love this book.

WEAPON OF TYRANTS, THE LAST WAR: BOOK
FOUR, by Sylvie Grayson

*Fanny Master is running for her life. Can she trust a criminal enforcer
to keep her safe?*

The International Head Balls Games are about to begin
at Deep Creek. Tension rises with Adar Silva, Khandarken,
Jiran and Legitamia scheduled to take part. Damian Stuke, an
enforcer for a gamer in the Western Territory, still has
nightmares about being captured and tortured during the Last

War. When his sister marries the Chief Constable of Khandarken, his life has to change.

Training for undercover work in Deep Creek in the midst of the Games, he encounters a fascinating woman with a small child and a hidden agenda. But as he discovers what she's hiding, his protective instincts kick into high gear.

Fanny Master's her parents are assassinated, and she runs for her life. A member of the Khandarken elite, she doesn't know who is after he, but she'll do almost anything to remain under the radar. That could include using someone else's ident and adopting their child, a child who might be from another world.

As Emperor Carlton ramps up his plans for invasion, the assassin makes a new attempt on Fanny's life. Damian is her only hope. Will he save her from her unknown enemy, or is he still working for the other side?

The Last War has been a truly excellent series so far, and Weapon of Tyrants is staying strong. Exciting, full of intrigue and adventure, wonderfully developed strong lead characters with a great supporting cast, neat world-building and excellent writing. I mean, what more can you ask for? You do need to start with book 1, but it too was excellent so you can't go wrong, and I can guarantee you'll have a ball with this one.

Find Sylvie Grayson at www.sylviegrayson.com to subscribe to her newsletter.

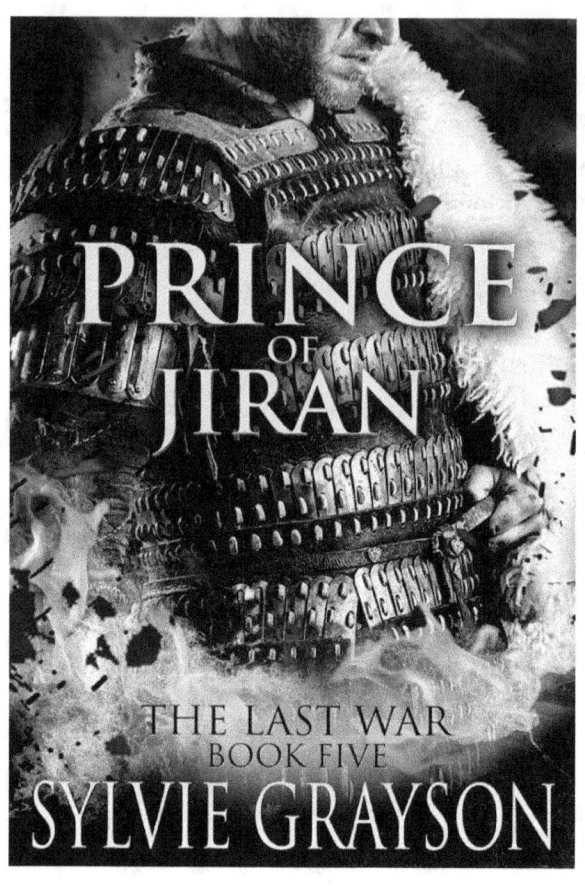

PRINCE OF JIRAN, THE LAST WAR: BOOK FIVE, by
Sylvie Grayson

*A Penrhy prince caught between duty and desire. Can he win the
impending battle?*

Shandro, Prince of the Penrhy tribe of Jiran, has a goal to
uphold the family values in spite of his father's conniving
moves as he deals with the hotbed of competing nations
surrounding them.

Then he's is sent on a mission across the mountains into Khandarken to bring back Princess Chinata, a bride for Emperor Carlton's Advisor. In exchange, Jiran and the Penrhy tribe are given a peace agreement, protection against invasion by the Emperor's troops. This seems a good trade, as Carlton is hovering on their borders with his need for more land. However, not far into the journey, it becomes apparent someone is not adhering to the terms of the peace accord.

Near the tribal border, Shandro and his troops have come under direct attack from unknown forces. He digs deeper into Chinata's background to find strong ties to the New Empire. Is it too dangerous to bring Princess Chinata into Jiran? Or as her escort, does Shandro become her defender against the Emperor's troops?

BANDEROS, THE LAST WAR: BOOK SIX, by Sylvie Grayson

Loyal Hawker must protect Angel any way he can from her brothers' ruthless ambitions.

Loyal Hawker, an undercover agent for the Khandarken military, has never met anyone quite like the woman he encounters on his trip to the south. He's approached by Angel, only daughter among the many sons of Gerwal Banderos, a well-known strongman who seized much of the unclaimed territory north of Adar Silva at the end of the Last

War. Angel declares her father wants to meet with him on a matter of urgency. While suspicious of her intentions as she leads him across extensive territory toward the Banderos compound, Loyal can't deny his attraction to her.

With Emperor Carlton invading in an attempt to reclaim his Empire, danger hovers over the Banderos land, and the brothers show they're not as united as they first appear. During the ensuing chaos, when the compound is besieged, Loyal must work in the midst of deceit and betrayal to protect what is left of Angel's heritage. Can he survive long enough to find out who's targeting Angel and save her from her treacherous brothers?

I was hooked with the first book, Khandarken Rising, The Last War: Book One, and will continue to read each subsequent novel. The action is continuous from the beginning thru the end of each book. In addition to a fine story in a differing world, with succinct writing, there are also supernatural incidences that pop up throughout the series that add just a touch of spice. Five stars. Amazon reader

ABOUT THE AUTHOR

Sylvie Grayson has published romantic suspense novels, *Suspended Animation, Legal Obstruction, The Lies He Told Me: Book One, Rain Man, Lies He Told: Book Two, Don't Move, Lies He Told: Book Three, False Confession, My Best Mistake, Dead Wrong,* all about strong women who meet with dangerous odds, stories of tension and attraction.

She has also written *The Last War* series *Khandarken Rising, Son of the Emperor, Truth and Treachery, Weapon of Tyrants, Prince of Jiran, Banderos, The Last Sovereign,* a romantic suspense sci/fi – fantasy series set in a new world she has created. She has been an English language instructor, a nightclub manager, an auto shop bookkeeper and a lawyer. She is a wife and mother, and lives in southern British Columbia with her husband on a small piece of land near the Pacific Ocean that they call home, when she's not travelling the world looking for adventure.

Follow her here— www.sylviegrayson.com

https://www.facebook.com/sylvie.grayson

https://www.bookbub.com/profile/sylvie-grayson

sylviegraysonauthor@gmail.com

www.ingramcontent.com/pod-product-compliance
Lightning Source LLC
Chambersburg PA
CBHW051938220626
47052CB00004B/701